ABOU

Barbara Cartland, the w
ist, who is also an hist
speaker and television p
books and sold over 50(

She has also had many
written four autobiographies as well as the biographies of her
mother and that of her brother, Ronald Cartland, who was
the first Member of Parliament to be killed in the last war.
This book has a preface by Sir Winston Churchill and has just
been republished with an introduction by the late Sir Arthur
Bryant.

"Love at the Helm" a novel written with the help and
inspiration of the late Earl Mountbatten of Burma, Great
Uncle of His Royal Highness The Prince of Wales, is being
sold for the Mountbatten Memorial Trust.

She has broken the world record for the last fifteen years by
writing an average of twenty-three books a year. In the
Guinness Book of Records she is listed as the world's
top-selling author.

Miss Cartland in 1978 sang an Album of Love Songs with
the Royal Philharmonic orchestra.

In private life Barbara Cartland, who is a Dame of Grace of
the Order of St. John of Jerusalem, Chairman of the St. John
Council in Hertfordshire and Deputy President of the St.
John Ambulance Brigade, has fought for better conditions
and salaries for Midwives and Nurses.

She championed the cause for the Elderly in 1956 invoking
a Government Enquiry into the "Housing Conditions of Old
People".

In 1962 she had the Law of England changed so that Local
Authorities had to provide camps for their own Gypsies. This
has meant that since then thousands and thousands of Gypsy
children have been able to go to School which they had never
been able to do in the past, as their caravans were moved
every twenty-four hours by the Police.

There are now fourteen camps in Hertfordshire and Barbara Cartland has her own Romany Gypsy Camp called
Barbaraville by the Gypsies.

Her designs "Decorating with Love" are being sold all over

the U.S.A. and the National Home Fashions League made her in 1981, "Woman of Achievement".

Barbara Cartland's book "Getting Older, Growing Younger" has been published in Great Britain and the U.S.A. and her fifth Cookery Book, "The Romance of Food" is now being used by the House of Commons.

In 1984 she received at Kennedy Airport, America's Bishop Wright Air Industry Award for her contribution to the development of aviation. In 1931 she and two R.A.F. Officers thought of, and carried the first aeroplane-towed glider air-mail.

During the War she was Chief Lady Welfare Officer in Bedfordshire looking after 20,000 Service men and women. She thought of having a pool of Wedding Dresses at the War Office so a Service Bride could hire a gown for the day.

She bought 1,000 secondhand gowns without coupons for the A.T.S., the W.A.A.F.s and the W.R.E.N.S. In 1945 Barbara Cartland received the Certificate of Merit from Eastern Command.

In 1964 Barbara Cartland founded the National Association for Health of which she is the President, as a front for all the Health Stores and for any product made as alternative medicine.

This has now a £650,000,000 turnover a year, with one third going in export.

In January 1988 she received "La Medaille de Vermeil de la Ville de Paris", (the Gold Medal of Paris). This is the highest award to be given by the City of Paris for ACHIEVEMENT – 25 million books sold in France.

In March 1988 Barbara Cartland was asked by the Indian Government to open their Health Resort outside Delhi. This is almost the largest Health Resort in the world.

Barbara Cartland was received with great enthusiasm by her fans, who also fêted her at a Reception in the city and she received the gift of an embossed plate from the Government.

A Theatre of Love

The Duke of Moorminster goes to the country to escape the persistence of his mistress Lady Fiona Faversham, who wishes to marry him.

While he is riding alone over his estate he hears the organ of a small Church being exquisitely played.

Curious he dismounts and goes in to find a number of children singing a Christmas Carol while their teacher a very young and beautiful girl has the most unusually clear and wonderful voice.

He decides that the girl who looks like an Angel and the small children should perform on his private Theatre which he has just finished building in Moor Park which is his Ancestral home.

How the Duke discovers that the whole of the small village is unexpectedly musical.

How he writes a performance for the opening of his Theatre at which the Prince and Princess of Wales are to be present.

How in doing so he finds something very precious that he has looked for all his life, is told in this unusual and very attractive 448th book by Barbara Cartland.

BARBARA CARTLAND

A Theatre
of Love

Mandarin

A THEATRE OF LOVE

First published in Great Britain 1991
by Mandarin Paperbacks
Michelin House, 81 Fulham Road, London SW3 6RB

Mandarin is an imprint of the Octopus Publishing Group

Copyright © Cartland Promotions 1991

A CIP catalogue record for this title
is available from the British Library
ISBN 0 7493 0744 7 PB
ISBN 0 7493 0845 1 HB

Printed and bound in Great Britain
by Cox & Wyman Ltd, Reading, Berks.

AUTHOR'S NOTE

It seems extraordinary that there is no book written about the many attractive and fascinating private theatres which existed in the last two centuries over the world.

There is still one to be seen in the Winter Palace in Leningrad and Prince Ysvolsov's Private Theatre is exactly as I described it in this book.

The Esterhazys' Palace in Hungary, not only had a Puppet Theatre, but also an Opera House. This unfortunately was burnt down and never rebuilt.

In big houses in England there were Christmas Traditions that were carried out by every generation.

Most of them had the present giving which I have written about here and I remember my Grandmother always gave every woman they employed in the house and on the Estate, enough red flannel to make a petticoat.

I used to think that perhaps some of them would have liked to have another colour.

Bell-ringers I remember coming to my Great-Uncle's house where we spent Christmas and I was fascinated by the beautiful tunes they extracted from their bells.

"*God Rest Ye Merry, Gentlemen*" is one of the oldest English Carols known.

It was sung in the open air like the first great Christmas Carol in Judea and the tune was a particular favourite of the strolling bands of minstrels.

Children sang it going from door to door in the hope of receiving a small coin, an orange or a mincepie.

Chapter One
1879

The Duke of Moorminster arrived back in England in a bad temper.

It had been a very tiring trip to Holland where he had been at the request of the Queen and the Prime Minister.

If there was one thing he found boring it was the speeches made by Statesmen who looked like Burgomasters.

Also those made by Bergomasters who looked exactly like the portraits of their ancestors in the Rijksmuseum.

He wondered as he listened if anything eventually evolved from such long-winded platitudes.

However, by what he considered extreme good luck, he was able to leave Holland a day earlier than he expected.

He therefore, through the British Embassy, cabled to London to alert his staff.

He knew, if nothing else, he would have a good dinner on his return.

Fate was however against him as the ship leaving from Rotterdam was delayed and the voyage was extremely rough.

The Duke was a good sailor, but it was raining and far too cold to go out on deck.

He was therefore confined to a cabin which he thought scornfully was too small for a rabbit-hutch.

It was some consolation when he stepped ashore at London Dock to find his own carriage drawn by two of his well-bred horses waiting for him.

Also his Secretary was there to see to the luggage.

Having greeted Mr. Watson, he drove off intent only on reaching his house in Grosvenor Square and having a hot bath.

It was far later than he had intended and he was therefore hungry.

Even the glass of champagne which his Butler had ready for him and some *pâté de foie gras* sandwiches did not entirely change his mood.

When he went up to his room he was frowning.

The footman who was there to valet him until his own Valet arrived with his luggage, looked at him apprehensively.

Mr. Watson had left the more urgent of the letters awaiting the Duke on his chest-of-drawers.

There were only a few of them.

The Duke knew that there would be a large pile downstairs in his Study.

He had no intention of reading them until tomorrow.

He looked at those on his chest-of-drawers and saw there was one in a blue envelope.

He recognised the hand-writing, as Watson had done and had therefore not opened it.

The Duke put the other letters aside and slitting open the envelope drew out a note from Fiona Faversham.

He knew before he even read it that it was a letter to welcome him home.

She had, of course, expected that he would receive it tomorrow.

Lady Faversham was now so much a part of his life

that he wondered sometimes why she troubled to write to him.

While he was away in Holland he had received a letter from her almost every day.

It seemed unnecessary now for her to write welcoming him home.

She undoubtedly expected him to be with her tomorrow evening.

Then when he read the endearments with which she started her letter he knew the reason.

It was all too obvious for him to question it.

Fiona wished to marry him.

It was in fact assumed by most of their friends that that was what he would eventually do.

Nearly thirty-four, the Duke was well aware that his whole family thought it was time he produced an heir.

They continually hinted that it was in fact his duty.

They were prepared to welcome Fiona with open arms.

She was one of the most beautiful women in England and they all believed he was infatuated with her.

She was also the daughter of the Duke of Cumbria.

The only stumbling-block in all this was that the Duke himself had no wish to be married.

If he had to be, he preferred to choose his wife irrespective of anybody else's ideas.

He certainly did not wish to be pressured up the aisle by people who, he thought, should mind their own business.

That included his whole family.

He carried out his duties as he was expected to do where it concerned the innumerable Uncles, Aunts, and an amazing number of Cousins.

But he disliked their presuming on their relationship or interfering in his private life.

11

It was true he found Fiona Faversham very attractive. When she had burst on London when her days of mourning were over he had found it impossible to resist her.

She had been married when she was not quite eighteen to Lord Faversham.

He not only came from one of the oldest families in England, but was at the time extremely wealthy.

He was also a very attractive man.

Someone had remarked that he had enjoyed more love-affairs than most people had hot dinners.

He had fallen wildly in love with Fiona.

He had swept her off her feet and beguiled her family into believing he would 'turn over a new leaf'.

Human nature being what it is, he did nothing of the sort.

After a honeymoon visiting all the romantic places in Europe he had returned to England with his Bride.

He had then taken up his life from where it had left off.

The trouble was that Eric Faversham could not resist a pretty face.

"It really means nothing, darling," he had said to Fiona.

She had caught him out spending the night with a woman whose beauty embellished the pages of the magazines and newspapers.

"But you have been unfaithful to me!" Fiona had protested plaintively.

"I love you, and I promise you that what I felt for Isobel was no more important than drinking a glass of champagne!"

Unfortunately as the years passed the "glasses of champagne" multiplied.

Fiona was asserting that she could stand no more of it when Eric Faversham was killed.

He was taking part in a Steeple-Chase in which all the riders had wined and dined too well.

Because some idiotic member of the party had dared them to do so, they had ridden after dinner.

They wore their evening-clothes with one eye covered with a black patch.

Several riders in the race had suffered injuries and two horses had had to be destroyed.

Eric Faversham had broken his neck and died instantly.

Fiona had not pretended to grieve for him.

His numerous love-affairs had humiliated her.

It hurt her to know she could not hold her husband.

Yet her beauty which had improved with age, sent other men into ecstasies.

She had retired to her father's house in the country for the conventional year of mourning.

Queen Victoria would not have approved of it being shortened in any way.

Fiona was sensible enough to return to London only when she had put away the last of her mauve and grey gowns.

Anyway they had not become her half so well as when she had worn black.

Because her hair was red, the deep red of Hungarian women, her skin was dazzlingly white.

Her eyes were not the clear green they should have been with such colouring.

At the same time, once a man had looked deeply into them he felt as if he had fallen into a whirlpool.

There was no chance of being saved.

13

To say that Fiona caused a sensation in London Society was to describe it mildly.

At twenty-five she was no longer the innocent unsophisticated girl she had been when she first married.

Her husband had taught her about love.

She had also learnt a lot from the women he had likened to "glasses of champagne".

Fiona made up her mind that her second marriage would be very different from her first.

Apart from anything else, she discovered after Eric's death that he had left a mountain of debts and was not nearly as wealthy as both she and her parents had been led to believe.

He had been wildly extravagant in the way he lived, especially in the parties he gave.

Besides this he was unnecessarily generous to the women he favoured and at the same time a compulsive gambler.

There was enough money left for Fiona to be comfortable.

But it was not the fortune she had anticipated.

She knew however, she wanted a position in Society second only to Royalty.

She also desired a husband who was wealthy enough to indulge her every whim.

There was only one man who fulfilled these requirements.

One man who was also attractive enough to make her heart beat faster.

He was the Duke of Moorminster.

When almost by instinct they gravitated towards each other the first time they met, she thought she had won the 'Jackpot'.

14

The difficulty was to persuade him to say the five magical words – "Will you be my wife?"

As it happened, the Duke was well aware of Fiona's intentions from the first.

He had been angled for, pursued and seduced by every woman he met from the moment he left Eton.

He would have been very stupid not to be aware he was the biggest matrimonial catch in the country.

He had learned to recognise the danger-signals even before he was forced to confront them.

He had grown adept at managing to avoid the more obvious traps set for him by ambitious mothers.

He found Fiona amusing, witty, and very sure of herself in a way he appreciated.

They were in fact two of a kind.

When he became her lover he found he had to exert himself – which was unusual – in order to dominate the situation as he was accustomed to do.

She was compliant and, as somebody had said, they "talked the same language".

He therefore found it easy to enjoy a situation which he felt confident he could control.

He allowed Fiona to become part of his life.

In London they saw each other almost every day.

They were invited to the same parties, and if he gave one himself she played hostess.

When he went to the country the same thing happened.

Having helped him choose the guests, Fiona came with him.

She made everything during the week or week-end pass smoothly and most enjoyably.

He hardly noticed when she moved her bedroom next to his because it was "more convenient".

He had taken it for granted that they would dine together the following night when he had expected to return from Holland.

It was actually an oversight – or perhaps for once he was being a little more cautious.

But he had neglected to instruct his Secretary in his cablegram to inform Lady Faversham that he was to return earlier than expected.

He went down to dinner.

He thought with a large Dining-Room it would have been pleasant to have her sitting beside him.

She would be telling all that had happened while he had been away.

He knew she would be amusing, and he knew too there would be a lot to hear.

Who the Prince of Wales was courting, who had quarrelled with women.

And of course what new *affaires de coeur* were taking place amongst their intimate friends.

It was actually very unusual for the Duke to dine alone.

Because the silence was somewhat oppressive he talked to his Butler as he and two footmen served the meal.

Redding, who had been with him for many years, was closely in touch with the servants at Moor Park.

The Duke therefore learnt what were the prospects for a good bag at the shoot he had arranged for Boxing Day.

He also learnt how good the hunting had been since he had been away.

"They'd an excellent run on Saturday, Your Grace," Redding was saying, "an' a kill in Bluebell Wood just afore they reached th' pool."

The Duke knew exactly where that was, and wished he had been there.

Redding put a small glass of brandy beside him because he never drank port.

"Is there anything more, Your Grace?" Redding enquired respectfully.

"See that I am called early tomorrow morning," the Duke ordered. "I will have a lot of correspondence to see to."

"Very good, Your Grace."

Redding bowed and went from the Dining-Room.

The Duke sat back in his chair and sipped his brandy.

As he did so he wished again that Fiona was with him.

"I will see her tomorrow," he told himself.

He had had enough time in Rotterdam to buy her a very attractive and expensive present.

He had intended to give it to her for Christmas, but now he thought she might as well have it at once.

There was only a little over a week to Christmas.

The thought made him remember that he had something to do at Moor Park besides hunting.

He had long ago made up his mind to rebuild the private Theatre.

It had originally been built in the 18th century only to be burnt down in the reign of William IV.

His ancestors had possessed many talents and outstanding qualities.

But none of them had any desire to express themselves either in music or in writing.

Quite unexpectedly the Duke had found himself proficient in both.

While his contemporaries appraised the women on the stage of the theatre, he criticised the Play itself.

Often he felt he could have done better.

To the astonishment of his relations he had started to rebuild the small Theatre at Moor Park.

He intended to restore it as it had been originally.

He had been lucky in this because to his delight he had found the original plans.

They had been drawn up by superlative Architects who had also been responsible for redesigning the house itself.

They had made what had been a "hotch-potch" of many preceding generations into a magnificent building. It was acclaimed as being architecturally perfect.

The facade they created was Georgian, but they had been clever enough to preserve behind it many of the rooms, exactly as they had been originally.

This included the Chapel.

The site where the Theatre had stood had fortunately remained unbuilt-upon.

Having found the original plans, the Duke proceeded to follow them exactly.

The Theatre was almost finished the last time he had been to Moor Park.

If he went home at the end of the week, he would see it completed.

Because he had been so pleased with its reconstruction he had told the Prince of Wales about it, who had said:

"You must certainly invite me to your Opening Performance, Sheldon."

He had paused to think, adding:

"We will spend Christmas at Sandringham, and if you remember, Christmas Day is on a Wednesday this year. The Princess and I will come to Moor Park the following

Friday, and you can have your Opening Performance on Saturday night."

"There is nothing, Sir, that will give me greater pleasure," the Duke replied, "and I will try to produce something unique."

"And of course beautiful!" the Prince had added.

That, the Duke thought, went without saying, knowing the Prince had an eye for any pretty woman.

He also enjoyed the Theatre and had shown that when he had courted Lily Langtry.

When this affair was over he had bestowed on her a fame she would never have had without him.

The Duke thought now that he had only two weeks in which to arrange, as he had promised the Prince, "something unique".

The "beautiful" would not be so difficult, were it not that Princess Alexandra would be present.

That meant that the cast on the stage could not include the Ballet Dancers from Covent Garden, or the undoubted Beauties of Drury Lane.

In a bachelor party it would have been quite easy for them to stay in the house.

After their performance they would amuse the audience in the way which would be expected.

The Duke had been intent primarily on the restoration of the building.

After this conversation with the Prince, he had had no time to consider who should appear on his Opening Night.

Now, he told himself, he had to get busy, and of course Fiona would help him.

He recalled that when he had mentioned it to her before, she had claimed surprisingly that she had a very good voice.

19

He must, she added, think up some scene in which she could sing for him.

When he questioned her she had explained.

"When I was at home we always used to act a Play of some sort for Papa at Christmas and on his birthday."

"Did you have a Theatre of your own?" the Duke asked.

"No, we used to do them in the Ball-Room, and the Estate carpenter fixed up a curtain for us and provided a backdrop."

She smiled before she went on:

"It would be very exciting to sing in a real Theatre with footlights!"

She looked up at him archly and added:

"I have always thought that if I had not been who I am, I could have had great success on the 'boards'."

"I am sure you would have, seeing how beautiful you are!" the Duke replied because it was expected of him.

"I am sure I would have been another Mrs. Siddons," Fiona had gone on, "and instead of acting a part just for you, my dearest Sheldon, I might have been performing to a full house at Drury Lane!"

"I think you would have found it somewhat arduous," the Duke remarked dryly.

He had had various brief affairs with actresses and dancers.

He was well aware that backstage was very different from the glamour that was seen from the front.

Now he knew he had no time to write anything for Fiona.

Instead he would engage Professionals.

They would include Musicians and famous Singers whom Princess Alexandra would appreciate.

The Duke knew exactly what the Prince's taste was.

But that would be impossible to cater for at what would be a family party.

There was no question of his grandmother who was over seventy, not being there.

If the Christmas house-party stayed on for the Performance as they would insist on doing there would be innumerable other relatives who would all be extremely critical.

They would also be shocked at anything that might be considered vulgar.

The Duke began to realise the whole idea was much more difficult than he had expected,

"I must talk to Fiona about it," he told himself.

He was quite certain she would find a solution.

If not, she would know exactly the people to whom they could turn for assistance.

He was not aware himself how much he had grown to depend on her.

When he thought about it, however, he knew she was making herself indispensable for her own ends.

As he rose from the table having finished his brandy, another idea occurred to him.

Perhaps after all he might as well marry Fiona and get it over with.

She could be ready to take over all the running of the house.

He could concentrate on the estate.

The horses, the pheasants, the farms, the livestock.

Also the great number of people whose lives he controlled because their families had served his for generations.

He walked from the Dining-Room.

Then as he was moving towards his Study he had a sudden thought.

His present for Fiona was upstairs, and there was no reason why he should not take it to her now.

She would be astonished to see him, but she would be very thrilled.

She had made that clear in the letter he had read before he had had his bath.

She had written:

"I am counting the hours until Thursday. Last night I spent a very dreary dinner with the Burchingtons who were quarrelling as usual. I have no plans for tomorrow night, but will just sit counting the hours until I can see you again.

The joy and excitement of it will be overwhelming as it seems like a century since you went to Holland.

I want to be close to you, I want you to tell me that you have missed me, and I want, my most handsome, adorable man, things which it would be a mistake for me to write down."

She signed her name with a flourish and the Duke knew exactly what she wanted.

He wondered if in fact he was too tired.

Then he asked himself how he could even think such a thing at his age.

Half the men in London would give their right arm to be Fiona's lover.

He went up the stairs to collect the bracelet he had bought for her in Amsterdam.

An Equerry to the Queen had been only too willing to tell him the name of the most reliable Jeweller in the City.

22

The Merchant had produced a bracelet, which the Duke saw was set with extremely fine blue-white diamonds.

He had also shown him a ring which he said he was selling for a Client.

It had a single diamond cut in the shape of a heart.

"It is an exceptionally fine stone, Your Grace," the Merchant said, "and it would be very hard to find another comparable to it."

Turning it over and over so that it caught the light the Duke had known this was the truth.

It struck him because it was heart-shaped that it would make a perfect engagement-ring when he did decide to marry.

The family jewels were magnificent.

When his mother appeared at the Opening of Parliament, she had always been more resplendent than any of the other Peeresses.

Now most of the jewels were in the safe awaiting the moment when he had a wife.

There were, he knew, several engagement-rings that had been passed down from generation to generation.

He had always understood however that a fiancée was given a ring to be her own and not part of the family collection.

Finally, the Duke had bought both the bracelet and the ring.

They were expensive, but he felt he had obtained, as the Equerry had promised, his "money's worth".

As he put the bracelet into his pocket he left the ring in the drawer.

If he did propose to Fiona, it would be waiting for her.

But he had not yet fully made up his mind.

23

He did not know why, except that she had pursued him so ardently.

He felt as if the whole thing was contrived and, at the same time, too obvious.

He did not know exactly what he did want, except of course that his wife must be beautiful.

All the previous Duchesses of Moorminster had been that.

Of course too her blood must be the equal of his.

That condition was certainly satisfied where Fiona was concerned because her father's Dukedom was older than his.

He wanted somebody who excited him physically.

She must also grace the position she would hold in the same way that his own mother had done.

He remembered when he was a small boy peeping from the Minstrels' gallery at a dinner-party taking place in the Banqueting Hall.

He had thought his father at one end of the table looked like a King.

His mother at the other end looked like a Fairy Princess.

She glittered with every move she made and she was the most beautiful woman present.

Fiona would certainly be that.

It crossed his mind that perhaps she would not be loved as his mother had been.

She was still adored by the servants on the estate.

"T'Duchess be a angel come down from 'eaven to be among us!" he remembered one of the old pensioners saying.

He had been only a small boy at the time but it was something he had never forgotten.

Fiona was certainly no angel.

In fact in the fiery encounters of their love she might be more appropriately described as coming from the fires of Hell.

That sounded somewhat derogatory, but the Duke was smiling.

There was a glint in his eyes that had not been there before.

He wanted Fiona, he wanted her now, and she lived only just around the corner.

Her house was in Carlos Place.

To reach her he had only to brave the elements for a few minutes.

When he reached the hall a footman had his sable-lined coat ready for him.

It had an astrakhan collar to keep his neck warm.

Another footman handed him his tall hat and his gloves.

A third supplied him with a cane.

"You are quite certain, Your Grace, you do not require a carriage?" the Butler asked respectfully.

"No, thank you, Redding, I am not going far," the Duke replied.

There was a knowing look in the man's eyes which the Duke did not see.

The front door was opened, and the Duke walked rather carefully down the steps in case they were slippery with frost.

There was certainly going to be a sharp one tonight, he thought.

Outside it was extremely cold.

The Duke walked quickly and was glad there was no wind.

Carriages were moving through the Square.

In the house next door to his there had obviously been a dinner-party, and the guests were now leaving.

The Duke moved quickly past them in case he should be recognised.

Then he turned into Carlos Place.

Fiona had an attractive house on the left-hand side.

The Duke knew it so well that he thought he could have found his way there blindfold.

As he went up the steps he felt for the key which had been in the drawer in his bedroom.

On one thing he had been very particular.

He had never allowed Fiona to come to his house in Grosvenor Square alone at night.

She did not dine there without a chaperon, nor would he make love to her after his other guests had departed.

"How can you be so pompous?" she teased him.

"I am protecting your reputation," the Duke had replied, "for, as you well know, servants talk."

She shrugged her shoulders, and it was a very pretty gesture.

"Does that really matter to us?"

"I think it does," he said quietly.

She had been slightly petulant about it.

Because he raised no objections about coming to her, she had given him the latch-key.

"I have no footman sitting up and watching who comes and goes," she said.

Therefore, when they were in London the Duke had gone to her house.

It was sometimes very late, if he had been on duty at the Palace or had dined with the Prince of Wales.

She had always been waiting for him in her bedroom.

She looked exquisitely lovely with her red hair falling over her shoulders and her skin translucent as a pearl.

She usually had a surprise for him in one way or another.

Once she had greeted him wearing a necklace of black pearls and nothing else.

Another time it was one of emeralds and a narrow belt of the same stones round her small waist.

Tonight, the Duke was thinking, she would not be expecting him.

Therefore he would have the pleasure of hearing her cry of joy.

He expected she would jump out of bed and throw herself into his arms.

He inserted the key in the lock and found the hall was in darkness.

It was nearly midnight, and he was sure that Fiona would have gone to bed early.

She would be saving herself for tomorrow night.

Only when the stars were fading would he hurry back to be in his own bedroom.

At six o'clock the housemaids in their mob-caps and the footmen in their shirt-sleeves would start cleaning the house.

He took off his coat and put it down on a chair.

He knew it was there without even having to look for it.

His hat and his gloves followed.

In the faint light which came from the fanlight above the front door he could make out the banisters.

Holding onto them he moved quietly up the thick carpet.

He passed the Drawing-Room which extended over the whole of the First Floor.

He climbed the next flight to where her bedroom was situated.

He paused for a moment before he put out his hand towards the handle of the door.

As he did so he stiffened.

There was the sound of somebody speaking inside and the voice was that of a man.

For a moment the Duke thought he could not be hearing correctly.

Or that he must have come to the wrong house.

Then, as he knew to whom the voice belonged, he felt as if he had been turned to stone.

Chapter Two

The Duke was aware that it was his First Cousin Joscelyn Moore who was in bed with Fiona.

Joscelyn was one of his relatives for whom he had no liking.

He had learnt that as his Heir Presumptive he had tried to borrow money from the Usurers.

But because it was only on the chance of his becoming the 3rd Duke of Moorminster they had sent him away ignominiously.

The story had somehow reached the gossips and had been related to the Duke.

It told him that Joscelyn Moor once again was deeply in debt.

He would soon be trying to put pressure on him again to save the family and the heir from disgrace.

The Duke was not mistaken.

This time he had spoken to his Cousin very severely, saying he had been given already more than his fair share of what money was available.

Joscelyn had been furious at being lectured.

The Duke thought now that perhaps he was taking his revenge by seducing Fiona.

As it happened, Joscelyn was very much like Eric

Faversham in that he could not resist a pretty face.

His love affairs were so numerous that they had long since ceased to shock his relatives.

Tall, good-looking like all the Moores, he had that strange charisma which men disliked but women found irresistible.

The Duke's first impulse was to go into the room and confront them.

Then his brain told him that this would be undignified.

Moreover he had no right to make any claims on Fiona when he had not asked her to marry him.

To have thought about it was very different from saying the words she longed to hear.

She had professed her love for him so ardently that he had foolishly imagined that she was faithful to him.

At least for as long as he remained her lover.

He now thought cynically that perhaps Joscelyn was not the first man she had taken to her bed when he was not available.

As he stood there unable to make up his mind what to do, he heard Joscelyn speak again.

"You are very lovely, Fiona," he said in a caressing tone, "and you will doubtless be the most beautiful Duchess of Moorminster whose portrait has ever hung in the Picture Gallery!"

"It is what I intend to be," Fiona replied. "At the same time, as you well know, it is not easy to make Sheldon talk of matrimony."

"Dammit!" Joscelyn swore. "He has to make an honest woman of you after getting you talked about by the whole of London."

"Perhaps you would like to tell him so?" Fiona replied mockingly.

"You know damned well he would not listen to me!" Joscelyn said, "and I will have to crawl on my stomach to make him pay my debts!"

"Oh, Joscelyn, are things as bad as that all over again?"

"Worse!" Joscelyn replied. "But Sheldon will have to pay up. Otherwise there will be an almighty scandal, and he will not like that!"

"You know, dearest Joscelyn, that I would help you if only I could, and when I marry Sheldon I will certainly make him more generous than he is at the moment."

The Duke clenched his fists.

He thought of the large amount of money he had given his Cousin.

It had all been thrown away on Actresses, prostitutes and his riotous friends.

To accuse him of not being generous was unforgivable.

He had already been forced to make economies on the Estate.

It was simply because Joscelyn had obtained large sums from him which could have provided wages and pensions for more workers.

Then he heard Fiona say:

"Do not let us talk of anything so depressing as money when we are close like this!"

"You are right," Joscelyn agreed, "and no one could be as soft, adorable and wildly exciting as you!"

There was silence, and the Duke knew that he was kissing her.

Slowly, carefully, so as not to make the slightest sound, he descended the stairs and reached the hall.

He put on his coat, picked up his hat and gloves and let himself out into the night.

31

As he walked home he was consumed with a fury that made him feel as if his whole body was on fire.

He knew if he was honest it was not only because Fiona had been unfaithful.

But that she should choose Joscelyn, of all men, with whom to do it was unforgivable.

He had talked to her, of course he had, of how abominably Joscelyn was behaving.

She had commiserated with him.

He knew however that as she did so, she was thinking that the answer to his problem was quite simple.

If he married and had an heir Joscelyn would no longer be able virtually to blackmail him.

That was what he was doing in making him pay his debts.

As Joscelyn had said, he could not allow his Heir Presumptive to go bankrupt.

The Duke entered his front door.

As he did so he knew decisively, without there being any further question about it, that he would never marry Fiona.

The Night-Footman, who was obviously surprised to see him back so soon, took his coat.

The Duke walked up the stairs to his bedroom.

He rang for his Valet, undressed without speaking, and got into bed.

When he was alone he lay in the darkness.

He felt that when he least expected it, the ceiling had fallen down on his head.

It was not that he minded so deeply that Fiona had taken a lover.

After all, as he told himself logically, she had every right to do so.

They were not tied to each other in any way.

At the same time, he had believed her continual pro-testations of love.

She had assured him over and over again that he was the only man in her life.

She had re-iterated a thousand times that she had never known such ecstasy as he had given her.

He had believed her, of course he had, because he wanted to.

And in fact, it was what a number of other women had told him.

Now he knew he had been a fool to think that such a thing was possible.

Fiona's husband had been a rake and a womaniser, and Joscelyn was the same.

Was it likely therefore that she could possibly be the innocent pupil she pretended to be?

The Duke had always prided himself on his intelligence.

He was indispensable to the Queen not merely because of his title and the fact that he was so handsome.

Granted it was well known that Queen Victoria liked handsome men.

She certainly had a "soft spot" in her heart for him.

But she also appreciated his brain.

She had often praised the way he could, when it was required, manipulate a Foreign Diplomat into agreeing to what she wanted.

When Lord Beaconsfield was Prime Minister he had said much the same thing.

"I can always trust Your Grace," he had said on one occasion, "to get your own way, which is my way, and I am very grateful."

The Duke had also believed in his infallibility when it came to ferreting out the truth.

He made sure he was not deceived in any way.

Yet Fiona had managed to deceive him.

He thought now he had been as stupid as a country yokel.

The question was, what did he intend to do about it?

For a start he had no intention of letting either Fiona or Joscelyn be aware that he had crept into her house and listened outside her bedroom door.

That would savour too much of the Servants' Hall.

It would make him appear undignified and even more foolish than he felt already.

Several hours of the night had passed before he finally made up his mind.

First, that neither Fiona nor Joscelyn should have the slightest idea that their behaviour had been discovered.

Secondy, that he would slowly manoeuvre Fiona out of his life.

He would do it subtly.

She would not be able to complain of his cruelty or give the clacking tongues of Mayfair anything to talk about.

He was not yet certain of how it should be done.

It was however, something he was determined to do.

At least he knew that he could not bear to see her the next evening as they had arranged.

If they dined together, she would inevitably want to console him for the nights he had spent without her.

He would find himself in the same bed which at the moment was occupied by Joscelyn.

The mere idea revolted him.

It was something which must be avoided at all costs.

Finally, before he fell asleep, he remembered he had told his Valet to call him at seven o'clock.

The Duke's Valet came into the room.

As he did so the Duke told him to inform Mr. Watson, his Secretary, that he was going to the country.

"To Moor Park, Y'Grace?" the man exclaimed in astonishment.

"Pack everything I shall need," the Duke ordered. "We will leave at ten o'clock."

By the time he was dressed and downstairs Mr. Watson was waiting for him.

"Good-morning, Your Grace!" he said. "I have been informed that you intend to leave for the country."

"That is what I have decided to do," the Duke replied as he walked towards the Breakfast-Room. "I have already sent my Assistant ahead to alert Moor Park to Your Grace's arrival," Mr. Watson said, "but I have of course no idea whether Your Grace is taking a party."

"I am going alone," the Duke said firmly.

Because he thought that Mr. Watson looked surprised he added as an afterthought:

"I want to see my Theatre. As you know, we have not yet decided who shall be the performers when their Royal Highnesses are present for the Opening."

"May I inform Your Grace that I have made out a list of the most distinguished singers available and there is also a Conjurer at one of the Music Halls who I am told is remarkable."

The Duke did not answer.

He was now sitting at the breakfast-table.

The Butler and two footmen were presenting him with the dishes that were kept hot on the sideboard.

Mr. Watson moved towards the door.

"I will join you in the Study," the Duke said, "when I have finished breakfast. Meanwhile, Watson, I shall want you to come with me to Moor Park."

What he said surprised Mr. Watson who seldom went with him to the country when the Duke had a party there.

He did not usually require his Secretary there.

He was he said, attempting to escape from the responsibilities which filled his life in London.

There were his duties at Buckingham Palace and Windsor Castle.

Heavy demands also were made on him by the Prince of Wales, sometimes officially and often as a friend.

His presence was often required by the Prime Minister.

He was requested by Ministers to attend innumerable Conferences and functions.

Especially those in which the Secretary of State for Foreign Affairs was concerned.

The Duke had spent a great deal of time in the last few years travelling to other countries.

Not only to countries in Europe, including Russia, but he had also been to America and Africa.

He had been of inestimable value to Ministers who had to rely on reports rather than see a situation for themselves.

The Duke went to his Study where Mr. Watson was waiting.

Apart from one pile of invitations which were undoubtedly social, there was another, that were of a Diplomatic nature.

He suspected there would be a third that were Political.

He seated himself at his desk and with a sweep of his hand said:

"You can bring all those with you. Is there anything urgent to which I should reply before we go?"

"There is a letter from His Royal Highness the Prince of Wales," Mr. Watson replied, "asking Your Grace to dine at Marlborough House tomorrow night, and saying that he would like to see you alone, if possible, tomorrow morning."

"You can send a note to the Prince," the Duke replied, "and everybody else saying that I have gone to the country on urgent matters concerning my Estate."

He paused a moment and then he continued:

"I will of course, contact His Royal Highness on my return."

Mr. Watson noted down what the Duke had said.

Then as there was silence he remarked somewhat tentatively:

"I think Your Grace is expected to dine with Lady Faversham this evening."

"Yes – of course!" the Duke said as if he had just thought of it. "Send Her Ladyship the same message, and all of them are to be delivered late this afternoon, which is when I was expected to return from Holland."

"Very good, Your Grace."

Mr. Watson hurried from the room.

The Duke sat back in his chair with a somewhat twisted smile at the corner of his mouth.

He knew that Fiona would be astonished and perhaps slightly perturbed.

Not only had he left for the country without seeing her first.

More significantly he had not written to her himself.

He had, he thought, struck the first blow in the campaign which would inevitably develop between them.

He knew she would fight like a tiger to keep him.

She would gradually become frantic when she discovered he was being elusive.

He expected there would be the usual tears and recriminations.

Such as had happened at the end of several of his *affaires de coeur*.

But they had never involved the possibility of marriage.

Fiona's position was therefore somewhat different.

He also expected she would inform Joscelyn who would call on him tomorrow.

He knew the tactics only too well.

As Joscelyn had said last night, he would beg him with heard-rending apologies for money.

If he was refused he would begin the familiar semi-blackmail, pointing out how much the family name would suffer.

He would emphasise how deeply distressed their relatives would be if his desperate situation should be reported in the newspapers.

Here he had a point.

The Press would not hesitate, as the Duke knew, to contrast the pitiable state of the Heir Presumptive with that of one of the wealthiest Dukes in the country.

The Duke's face was contorted as he brought his clenched fist down on the desk so violently that it made the ink-pots rattle.

"Curse him!" he exclaimed. "I shall have to pay up, and he knows it!"

He tried to tell himself that while there was nothing else

he could do, he should not allow Joscelyn's behaviour to upset him.

Yet when he left the Study there was a frown between his eyes.

There was no time to arrange for his Private Coach to be attached to the train on which he was to travel.

There was however, a Courier to escort him to the Station.

He would see that he was given a Reserved Carriage, and that the door was locked when he entered it.

Mr. Watson would be in the next coach and the luggage deposited in the Guard's Van.

There would be in fact, very little in the way of trunks.

The Duke had insisted on having a duplicate of everything he wished to wear in both of the houses in which he stayed most frequently.

He also had a house in Newmarket and another in Leicestershire.

There were therefore usually very few things to be conveyed from Grosvenor Square to Moor Park.

The most important this time were the letters which travelled beside Mr. Watson in a despatch-case.

The Courier acquired all the daily newspapers and put them in the Duke's carriage.

It was not a long journey as Moor Park was situated North of London in the most beautiful part of Oxfordshire.

It could be reached by road in under three hours.

The Duke however, in the Winter, found it much quicker and on the whole more comfortable to travel by train.

This would stop by request at his Private Halt.

He then had only a two-mile drive to his home.

As he stepped out of the train at The Halt there was a red carpet across the platform.

Three members of his staff were waiting for him.

Outside was a Chaise he liked to drive himself.

There was also a Brake in which to convey everybody else from the Station to the house.

He greeted those who were waiting for him in a somewhat frigid manner, which made them suspect that something was wrong.

Then he got into his Chaise, picked up the reins and drove off.

The Groom travelled in the seat at the back.

Therefore the Duke was not bothered by having the man beside him.

He drove his horses skilfully round the twisting lanes.

As he did, he thought that this was the first time for years that he had come home without a party to amuse him.

At the moment to be alone was all he wanted.

The austerity of it pleased him, just as he enjoyed the cold and frosty air on his cheeks and the greyness of the sky above.

He was not in the mood for sunshine or for the laughter and chatter of flirtatious women.

He wanted to be by himself, to "lick his wounds" before he moved up into the firing-line.

Moor Park was looking magnificent.

It did not matter whether it was Spring, Summer, Autumn or Winter.

The great house always looked the same.

The centre block with its wings reaching out on either side was breath-taking.

To the Duke it was everything that was stable in his

life – the foundation of his very existence.

He drove down the long drive.

As he did so he asked himself how he could have thought that Fiona Faversham could take the place of his mother, as the Duchess of Moorminster.

It was not only that she had deceived him.

He knew now that however beautiful she might be, both her character and her personality were wrong.

"If I married her and afterwards discovered her perfidy, it would have not only humiliated me, but smirched the whole history of the family," the Duke thought.

He crossed the ancient bridge over the lake that was as old as the house itself and drew up at the front door.

The red carpet was already down.

Footmen were waiting to open the door of the Chaise for him to alight.

The Butler was standing at the top of the steps.

It was all so familiar.

But the Duke had the feeling that he was seeing it for the first time.

Only now did he realise how much it meant to him.

He walked into the house and because he wanted to distract his mind he went immediately to where the Theatre was being rebuilt.

As he expected, the Architect and the Designer were waiting.

He went in through the door which connected the Theatre with the house.

When the Duke had found the plans drawn up by the Adam brothers he had also found a letter of instructions.

It had been written to them by his ancestor, then the 7th Earl of Moore.

It was his grandson, the 9th Earl who had distinguished

himself so gallantly under Wellington that he had been made a Marquis.

It was the Duke's father who had been raised to the Dukedom by Queen Victoria.

The Earl's instructions to the Adam brothers had been made after he had returned from a visit to Russia.

He had been there as a guest of the Tsar.

He told them that he had been exceedingly impressed by the Royal Theatre in the Winter Palace.

And even more so by Prince Ysvolsov's Private Theatre which was exceptional.

The Earl had managed to obtain sketches of the interior of the latter.

The Adam brothers had therefore been able to model their design on it exceedingly cleverly.

The Duke had last seen the Theatre a month before he left England to go to Holland.

He had been sure that his Architect and Designer could recreate the charm of the original Theatre at Moor Park.

He was however, a little apprehensive that he was expecting too much.

They were both waiting for him and led him through the door into the Theatre.

Because the house was on slightly higher ground than the foundations of the Theatre, the Duke found himself on a level with the boxes.

A flight of stairs in front of him went down into what in a Public Theatre would be known as the "Stalls".

The building was quite small, in fact it could hold few more than a hundred people.

It was, the Duke thought, like a child's doll's house.

Yet it had all the charm and beauty of what might have been a Royal Theatre.

42

In the Stalls were white and gold carved chairs.

The "Circle" was furnished with seats upholstered in crimson velvet.

The two boxes, one of which was intended for Royalty, had the same.

The whole effect was quite beautiful, as was the backdrop on the stage.

Curtains of rich red velvet were drawn back in front of the footlights.

There was a small 'Pit' for the Orchestra and a huge crystal chandelier hung from the ceiling.

The Architect and the Designer were watching the Duke's face.

He looked all round him in silence before he said:

"I congratulate you both! It is exactly what I wanted, and far better than I dared to expect!"

He knew by their looks before they spoke how gratified they were.

When he left them he walked back into the house to have a late luncheon.

For the first time since last night when he had stood outside Fiona's bedroom door, he could think of something else.

He knew he had to work quickly to decide which Prima Donna he should engage for the night the Prince of Wales would be in the audience.

More important, who should take part in the sketch he had half-written and which included a part for Fiona.

He had not realised until she insisted on singing for him, that she had a pleasant voice.

It was nothing exceptional.

But he knew that with her beauty it would not be difficult for her to have an appreciative audience.

Although it would in general be a critical one.

A great number of his relatives, including his grand-mother, came to Moor Park every Christmas.

They would have arrived without even receiving an invitation.

It was traditional that they should be there.

A tradition they had every intention of maintaining.

The idea had come to him that he would compose a song for Fiona in which she would appear as an angel.

But now he knew that to introduce Fiona as an angel would be a crime against God.

Then another idea came to him, and there was a melody in his mind that kept recurring.

He knew it would be with him until he had played it on the piano and transcribed it as a score.

He hoped that Fiona would not be staying with him at Christmas.

If she was, she would sit in the Stalls and watch somebody else play her part.

"You will not forget about the song I am to sing in your new Theatre?" she had asked the day before he was leaving for Holland. "I shall need time to practise it, and I know, darling, Sheldon, how you expect perfection."

"How could you be anything else?" he had said automatically because it was expected of him.

Now he told himself furiously that there was nothing perfect about Fiona.

"I will find somebody else for the part," he thought. "It should not be difficult."

After luncheon he ordered a horse from the stables.

As the Head Groom brought the horse to the front door, he predicted there would be snow before long.

"I doubt it!" the Duke replied curtly.

"We loiks t'have a white Christmas," the man remarked. "Las' year, if Y'Grace Remember, it never snowed 'til Boxin' Day!"

The Duke wondered what that proved.

He knew the staff at Moor Park, like his nieces and nephews, looked forward to snow at Christmas.

They were disappointed if they were denied it.

Because the Duke felt he must escape from his thoughts, he rode away over the fields.

He went Northwards passing through the woods he had not visited for a long time.

He knew that sometime he must talk to his game-keepers.

But for the moment he just wanted to be alone to be free of everything.

Most of all of his own feelings.

He rode on and on until he realised it was very cold and that soon it would be growing dark.

It was then he saw just ahead of him a small village that he had not visited for some years.

He remembered it was called "Little Bedlington".

It consisted of a few thatched cottages, an ancient black-and-white Inn, and what looked like a Norman Church.

There was still some left in the County.

The Duke thought dryly that most of the Churches on his estate were ceaselessly in need of urgent repairs.

He rode through the village looking at the thatch on the cottages which seemed to be in good repair.

The fences and gates were the same.

The few children he saw looked rosy-cheeked and well-fed.

He was just about to turn round and hurry home when he heard music coming from the Church.

For one moment he wondered why on a week-day anyone should be playing the organ.

Then as he drew his horse nearer he realised the playing was surprisingly skilful.

He knew only too well how heavy-handed some organists could be.

What he was listening to was an exceptionally beautiful rendering of a Carol "It Came Upon the Midnight Clear", and it brought back many memories.

As a Musician, which was what the Duke believed himself to be, he was impressed.

He could only commend the Organist for having a touch that was brilliant, and for knowing the way the Carol should be played.

He drew his horse up outside the Church door and sat listening.

As a child he had learnt that Carol and sung it to his mother.

The Organist finished it and stopped.

The Duke was curious as to who was playing.

He also felt that, as one Musician to another, he should congratulate the man.

He dismounted.

He tied the reins of his horse to an ancient post outside the porch and walked into the Church.

He found, as he had expected, that the Church was small.

The nave at any rate, was definitely Norman with its rounded arches and barrel roof.

His eye was caught by a particularly fine stained-glass window above the altar.

Then he became aware that seated in the carved stalls in the Chancel were a number of small children.

As he looked at them a young woman came from the organ behind them to stand in the centre of the aisle.

She was slight, and as he could see, very young.

She had an almost childlike face which was dominated by two large blue eyes.

Her hair which he could see from under her small bonnet, was fair.

It struck him that she had the appearance of an angel.

She stood still for a moment with her back to the altar.

Then she said to the children:

"Now that you have listened to the tune of that beautiful Carol, I want you to try to sing the words. I will sing them to you first, then you must follow me."

There was a little murmur from the children.

Lifting her head the girl, in a sweet, clear, very young voice began to sing.

As she did so the Duke realised that her voice was exactly what he might have expected from an angel.

There was something not human about it.

Something which seemed to have no connection with the world.

It could only come from Heaven where there was no sin, no unpleasantness, no horror, no fear.

He could not imagine why he should find himself thinking this.

Yet as the girl sang, and went on singing the thought came insistently into his mind.

It was almost as if somebody was saying the words to him.

She finished the first verse of the Carol.

The Duke was listening intently.

So, he was aware, were the children.

It was as if she had mesmerised them into silence.

As she finished she smiled and the Duke thought it was as if the sun had come out.

"Now we will do it to the music," she said.

She went back to the organ and the children, without being told, got to their feet.

Playing with the same exquisite touch which had drawn the Duke into the Church, she started the Carol once again.

This time her voice, as if she was "Star of Bethlehem" led the children.

They sang as only children can – with the freshness of youth, which was very moving in itself.

The Duke knew her voice was exceptional.

It was so true and pure that it could only be described as "angelic".

Chapter Three

When the children stopped singing the girl came from the organ and said:

"That was very good! Come tomorrow at the same time."

The children jumped up, eager to leave the Church.

They trooped past the Duke standing just inside the door, barely noticing him.

When they had gone he walked slowly up the aisle to where the girl was tidying away the Hymn Books.

As he reached her she looked up in surprise.

He thought that close to, she was even lovelier than she had appeared from a distance.

"Good-afternoon!" he said in his deep voice.

She smiled and replied:

"I thought I saw somebody at the back of the Church while we were singing."

"I heard you first playing the organ," he said, "and thought you had a professional touch."

She laughed and it was a very pretty sound.

"That is very complimentary, but I only started to play in the Church when the Organist died. My father, who is the Vicar, could not find a suitable replacement."

"I am sure nobody could play better than you do!" the Duke said.

She looked up at him with a shy little glance which told him she was not used to receiving compliments.

Then as she thought it was strange he was there she asked:

"Is there anything I can do for you?"

"I think there is," the Duke replied, "and I would like to discuss it with your father, who I imagine I met when he was first appointed to this Parish."

The girl was still, as if an idea had suddenly struck her.

Then she asked a little tentatively:

"You are not . . you cannot be . . ?"

"I am the Duke of Moorminster," he said, "and I was riding through the village when I heard you playing the organ."

The girl dropped him a curtsy.

"I am . . sorry," she said, "I . . I did not recognise you."

"There is no reason why you should," the Duke said, "and perhaps you would tell me your name?"

"It is Lavela Ashley, and my father has been the Vicar of Little Bedlington for nineteen years."

"In which case," the Duke said, "he was appointed by my father, so I would not know him."

"I am afraid Papa is not at home at the moment, but visiting a parishioner who is ill and lives some distance away."

The Duke thought for a moment. Then he said:

"I suggest that you and your father come to Moor Park tomorrow where I will discuss with you both something I would like you to do for me."

"Come to . . Moor Park?" Lavela Ashley asked in a low voice.

"At about eleven o'clock in the morning," the Duke said. "Have you some means of getting there?"

"Yes . . yes of course . . Your Grace."

"Then I shall be looking forward to seeing you, Miss Ashley, and may I say once again how much I enjoyed your playing."

Lavela curtsied and the Duke turned and walked down the aisle.

As he went he thought with satisfaction that at least he had found somebody to take the part of the angel in his Play.

She would certainly look like one.

He mounted his horse and rode off swiftly to get home before it was dark.

Riding fast because he knew the way, he was just able to manage it.

He rode up to the front door and saw there were servants looking out anxiously as if they wondered what had happened to him.

A groom was waiting at the bottom of the steps.

He went to his Study and took out the manuscript of the short Play he had not yet finished.

It had been copied out for him by Mr. Watson's assistant in excellent writing.

As the Duke read what he had written he knew he had had Fiona in his mind as he wrote it.

Slowly he tore it into pieces.

On one thing he was determined: Fiona should not act or sing in front of the Prince and Princess of Wales.

It occurred to him that she was anxious not only to do so because she liked showing off.

She might, if she found an opportunity, inveigle the Prince into helping her where their marriage was concerned.

It was well-known that the Prince, who was always in love with somebody, enjoyed assisting his friends with their love-affairs.

In fact on several occasions he had married off a hesitant Bridegroom.

He managed this simply by saying firmly to the man in question that he had already got the girl talked about.

"I did not intend to get married for at least another five years!" the Duke's friend had complained to him. "But what could I do with His Royal Highness hinting broadly that I would ruin Alice's reputation unless I proposed to her?"

The Duke thought his friend had been very foolish to have allowed himself to be trapped in such a manner.

He knew only too well that the Prince could never resist helping a pretty woman if she cried.

Too late he thought he should not have told Fiona that the Prince had invited himself to Moor Park.

It was not only a question of the Royal Couple.

All his family would be there, and there was no doubt that she would try to inveigle them into supporting her.

He had never thought of it before for the simple reason that he was determined that he would not be rushed into marriage.

He had forgotten how devious a woman could be when she wished to get her own way.

He decided he must somehow prevent Fiona from coming to stay.

It was going to be difficult because they had already discussed the party.

He knew that as usual, Fiona would more or less act as hostess, even if his grandmother was there.

"What shall I do?" he asked himself helplessly.

There was very little time before Christmas to hope that things might have changed before the party arrived.

If he dropped Fiona gradually, as he meant to do, sooner or later she would demand an explanation.

Then he would undoubtedly have to tell the truth.

"I shall just have to wait," he thought, "and see how things work out."

At the same time he was worried.

Having dined alone, he stayed up very late rewriting his Play.

A new idea had come to him.

It was Christmas and so many of his relatives were growing old.

He would write something which would make them feel that whatever their age, they were not forgotten.

They would be told there was still ways for them to help others and that they were needed.

He therefore envisaged the central figure as an elderly woman, regretting her lost youth.

He had already composed a song which she could sing.

She would regret the excitements, the joys, and the ambitions of youth.

Then because it was Christmas, a small child would bring her a present.

An older girl, also with a gift, would ask her help over a problem which concerned love.

At first the older woman would feel she did not know the answer.

Then she would give the girl the right one.

53

As the girl goes away happy to find the man she loves, the elderly woman would fall asleep.

While she was sleeping, she would dream.

An Angel appearing with two small cherubs would tell her there was no such thing as death.

Her good deeds would live on after she had left the world.

And even when she was in Heaven, she would still be helping and guiding those she loved.

When the idea had come to the Duke he had thought at first it was too sentimental.

Then he knew his grandmother and his aunts would love it.

It was in fact, something in which he genuinely believed, although he never talked about it.

The women in his life, including Fiona, he knew would have mocked at him if they thought he was religious.

They paid "lip-service" to the Church in that sometimes they attended a Service on Sunday.

They certainly appeared at every fashionable Wedding and Funeral.

The truth was that while they did so they were breaking the vows they had made when they married.

Besides most of the Commandments in one way or another.

He remembered one party at which Fiona was present when somebody had said jokingly to the woman with whom he was flirting:

"I am certainly breaking the Tenth Commandment in coveting my neighbour's wife!"

There was laughter at this and another wit had retorted:

"There is only one Commandment that matters, the eleventh: 'Thou shalt not be found out!' "

The Duke had laughed, and so had Fiona.

He thought now that she would have been shockingly miscast as an Angel.

He could not think of anyone who would really look angelic except the girl he had found today.

He wondered why he had never seen her before.

But there was no reason why he should have unless she had attended a Meet on this part of the Estate.

"Perhaps there is some more hidden talent amongst my tenants!" he thought with a smile.

He rose from his desk realising it was long after midnight.

He had written not a play but a very short episode with more music than words.

There still remained the music.

He thought he might incorporate part of the Carol which Lavela Ashley had sung so beautifully with the children in the Church.

Even as he thought of it he could see how it fitted in.

The music he had been composing himself would make a background for the Angel when she spoke to the old woman.

Perhaps he should write another song she could sing.

Because a tune was ringing in his brain he wanted to go to the Music Room and try it out on the piano immediately.

Then he knew that, in fact, he was very tired.

He had not slept much the night before, had risen early and ridden a long way during the afternoon.

He therefore went to bed.

Before he fell asleep he was again hearing Lavela's voice soaring up to the roof of the Norman Church.

He thought the pureness and clarity of it was different from any sound he had ever heard before.

The Duke awoke early and was humming to himself as he dressed.

After breakfast a horse was waiting for him outside the door and he rode for an hour.

He took all the jumps he had erected on his private race-course with such ease that he decided he should have them heightened a little.

He was back at the house at a quarter to eleven.

He had told the servants that he was expecting the Vicar of Little Bedlington and his daughter.

When they arrived they were to be shown into the Music Room.

This room, which was his favourite, was considered one of the most beautiful in the whole house.

White and gold, it had a painted ceiling of cupids with small harps while Venus in the centre of them was obviously singing an aria.

It had originally been painted by an Italian artist, but was in a bad state of repair when the Duke inherited.

His father who was not in the least musical never went into it.

The Duke as a boy had a piano in the School-Room.

When he grew older, there was one in the Sitting-Room which opened out of his bedroom.

One of the first things he had done when he became the reigning Duke was to open the Music Room.

He had it painted, gilded and the ceiling restored.

It now looked just as it had when the Adam brothers first designed it.

When he reached the Music Room he sat down at the piano.

He played, if not as well as a professional, very much better than the average amateur.

He had taken lessons from a great Concert Pianist when he was in Italy as a young man.

It was something he had never told anybody, thinking they would laugh at him.

In fact, very few people, even the women to whom he made love realised how much music meant to him.

Fiona had become aware of it simply because she was so often with him.

But he knew when he was playing to her one of his own compositions she was really thinking it would be much more enjoyable if she was in his arms.

The words with which she praised him were, he knew, spoken only to make him happy.

Not because she was convinced in her own mind that he was a good performer.

Now he propped a music score in front of him.

He began to note on it the tune which had come into his mind last night.

He had completed quite a lot when the door opened and a servant announced:

"The Reverend Andrew Ashley, Your Grace, and Miss Ashley!"

The Duke rose from the piano-stool.

He had been half-afraid this morning that he had been imagining things yesterday afternoon.

He had been convinced then that Lavela Ashley looked exactly like an Angel.

Perhaps he had been bemused by the music.

Perhaps because it was getting on in the afternoon and

the light was fading, his eyes had deceived him.

Now he took a quick glance at her before he looked at her father.

He saw that she was just as angelic in the pale sunshine coming through the window as he had thought her to be.

First he greeted the Vicar, an extremely handsome man as tall as the Duke himself.

He had clear-cut features and his hair was going grey at the temples.

There was moreover something distinguished about him which told the Duke he was a gentleman.

"I am delighted to meet you, Vicar," he said. "It is certainly very remiss of me that I have not done so before."

The Vicar smiled.

"We are at the far end of your Estate, Your Grace, and we live very quietly. I often think that Little Bedlington is forgotten."

"That is something which must be rectified in the future," the Duke replied.

He held out his hand to Lavela saying:

"I am so glad you have accepted my invitation and now I want to tell you what I have in mind."

The Duke walked towards one end of the room where he indicated a comfortable arm-chair for the Vicar.

He seated himself on the one opposite it while Lavela sat on the sofa.

"I expect your daughter has told you," the Duke began, "that quite by chance I was passing your Church yesterday afternoon. I heard her playing the organ and was extremely impressed at how well she did so."

"That is what I have always thought myself," the Vicar

58

replied, "and my wife is also very musical."

"Your daughter sang a Carol with the children," the Duke went on, "and I was aware she has a very unusual and lovely voice!"

He thought Lavela looked shy as he spoke and the colour came into her cheeks.

The bonnet she was wearing was the same one she had worn in Church.

She was also plainly dressed.

Yet it seemed somehow the right frame for her face with its huge eyes and child-like expression.

Once again the Duke could only describe her as "angelic".

In a few words he went on to explain to the Vicar and Lavela what he was planning for the Saturday after Christmas.

"I want to show you my Theatre," he said, "but first I would like your daughter to sing for me as I heard her yesterday in the Church."

"Of course, Your Grace," the Vicar said, "but we did not think of bringing any music with us."

"Never mind," the Duke said. "First I would like her to play and sing part of the Carol she was teaching her choir. Then I will tell her what else I would like her to do."

Without any mock humility or making any protestations, Lavela walked to the piano.

It was obvious she knew the Carol by heart.

In order to accustom herself to the keys, Lavela played a few bars of the tune alone.

Then she began to sing.

If the Duke had been moved by her voice yesterday, in the Music Room, where the acoustics were perfect, he was spellbound.

She finished the last two lines:

> *"The World in solemn stillness lay*
> *To hear the angels sing."*

He thought as she did so that anyone listening to her would be in "solemn stillness" as he was himself.

Lavela took her hands from the keyboard.

"I am sure, Your Grace," she said, "you do not want any more."

"I would like to hear the whole Carol," the Duke said, "but instead if you can read music, I want you to sing a few bars of something I have composed myself."

He handed her the score and sat down at the piano.

He ran his fingers over the keys, playing the melody so that she could hear it without the words.

Then he said:

"Now you try!"

He struck a chord.

Then as he waited, Lavela's voice exactly as he had envisaged it, turned his words into a sound that seemed to soar into the sky.

Once she hesitated, but otherwise she was able to read what he had written almost perfectly.

As she finished the Vicar clapped his hands.

"That was delightful, Your Grace!" he exclaimed. "I had no idea that you were a Musician!"

"It is something that most people do not expect of me," the Duke answered, "and when I was a boy I was too embarrassed to admit it."

"I think you should be very proud that you are able to compose anything so beautiful," Lavela said.

She was studying the music score as she spoke.

The Duke knew she was speaking in all sincerity and he smiled as he said:

"Perhaps one day, when we have time, I will show you some other pieces I have composed and the words I have put to them."

"That would be wonderful," Lavela said, "and very satisfying!"

The Duke was sure that any other woman would have said:

"And you could make a fortune selling them."

Instead he realised Lavela was thinking of how he would feel himself and what in fact, he did feel.

"Come and look at the Theatre," he suggested.

They went from the Music Room to the part of the great house where the Theatre was situated.

When he took them in through the door they stood at the top of the steps with the Royally furnished boxes on each side.

"It is magnificent!" the Vicar exclaimed. "I have often thought it was sad that the original Theatre was burnt down."

"You know about it?" the Duke asked.

"I have always been extremely interested in the history of the house, Your Grace, and your father was gracious enough to show me round himself, explaining the alterations that had been made in 1780 and the parts of the building that were left intact."

"That was a long time ago," the Duke said, "and I would like you to see what alterations have been made since."

"I would enjoy that more than I can say," the Vicar replied.

The Duke took Lavela up onto the stage.

She was as thrilled as Fiona would have been if he had given her a diamond bracelet.

"It is so small," the Duke said, "that I do not think you will feel nervous."

She smiled.

"I never feel nervous when we are acting a Nativity Play, which is what we give every Christmas in the School Hall."

She smiled at him before continuing:

"Of course here the audience will be different, but I expect I will be able to forget them."

"That is the right attitude," the Vicar said before the Duke could speak. "I always tell the children to try to think themselves into their parts, and really believe they are the Three Wise Men, the Shepherds, or the Virgin Mary Herself."

"I can see, Vicar, you have a flair for acting," the Duke remarked.

The Vicar laughed.

"I must admit that I enjoyed performing in a number of Plays when I was at Oxford."

"Papa is a very good actor," Lavela said, "One year, when we were very adventurous and put on *King Lear*, everybody said Papa was wasted as Vicar of Little Bedlington!"

"You are both making me feel that I have neglected my duties in not discovering all this hidden talent on my doorstep before now!" the Duke declared.

"Be careful!" Lavela warned him unexpectedly. "Once you start encouraging people to become actors and actresses there will be a great number who think they are brilliant performers but who are in fact lamentably bad, and it is very hard to get rid of them."

"That is very true," the Vicar agreed. "There are some elderly spinsters in my Parish who either wish to recite endless poems they have written themselves, or to sing, usually out of tune, on every possible occasion."

The Duke laughed.

"Thank you for warning me."

"When they hear about this beautiful Theatre," Lavela said. "You will have the greatest difficulty in discouraging them."

"Then I can only beg you not to talk about it," the Duke smiled.

"To be truthful that would be impossible," Lavela answered, "for even if we do not talk, everybody else will!"

"Everybody?" the Duke questions.

"There is nothing that happens at Moor Park which is not known and discussed simply because it is so exciting."

Lavela thought the Duke looked sceptical and explained;

"You, Your Grace, are our Landlord and also the most thrilling person in the whole Country."

"I suppose I should be flattered," the Duke said ruefully.

"When you give a party," Lavela went on, "every voice seems to rise in a crescendo!"

Her eyes were twinkling as she spoke and the Duke thought it made her look very pretty.

"Now you are definitely frightening me!" he objected. "I had no idea I was the chief topic of conversation!"

"But of course you are!" Lavela said. "Actually there is very little else to talk about except when a fox carries off a prize hen, or an otter is sighted in the river!"

"You paint a sad picture," the Duke laughed. "So I suppose I must not complain if my Theatre gives everyone a new topic."

"Which it certainly will!" Lavela said. "And of course, Your Grace, I am very . . very honoured to be . . allowed to . . sing in . . it."

She thought as she spoke that it was something she should have said before.

She glanced at her father as if she expected him to reprove her for having been so remiss.

"I can only say that I am delighted you have promised to play the part I wish you to do," the Duke assured her.

"I feel we should leave now, Your Grace," the Vicar said. "We have imposed for long enough on your time. If you will tell Lavela when you want her again, we will go home."

"As I am alone," the Duke said, "I would like you to have luncheon with me, and afterwards Vicar, I know my Curator will be delighted to show you round the house while I can run through with your daughter what she has to sing."

As he spoke he thought he would certainly enlarge Lavela's part.

Her voice was exceptional.

She must sing a solo either at the beginning of the Play or else at the end.

It was just an idea.

He wondered whether he was making her too important in a Show for which he had intended to engage a professional performer.

"If you are quite certain we are not imposing on Your Grace," the Vicar was saying, "Lavela and I will find that you suggest most enjoyable."

After luncheon the Vicar went off with the Curator to explore the house.

The Duke took Lavela into the Drawing-Room.

He had always thought himself that it was a very attractive room.

He knew by the way Lavela's eyes lit up and the way she gazed around her that to her it was a revelation.

The Duke was used to people who came to Moor Park for the first time being overwhelmed.

First by the sheer size of it, then by the way it was furnished and the treasures it contained.

It was, he thought, only his very sophisticated friends who took it all for granted.

The ladies were more concerned with the gowns their rivals were wearing.

The men were only interested in his horses.

When the Duke showed Lavela his priceless collection of snuff-boxes she looked at them in silence.

Then she said in a low voice as if speaking to herself:

"This is just like being in Aladdin's cave!"

Because she was so young and ingenuous the Duke exerted himself to show her several other rooms on the way to the Music Room.

He liked the way she admired everything without being over-effusive or gushing.

There was a light in her eyes that was more expressive than words.

When they reached the Music Room she said:

"Thank you . . thank you so very much for being so kind. Your house is exactly as I pictured it. I have often driven up the drive just to look at its beautiful façade and the statues on the roof."

It made the Duke think that it was many years since he had gone up onto the roof to look at the statues.

Because he had taken them for granted he had almost forgotten who they represented.

"Until Christmas," he said, "You will not only look at the house from the outside, but come in, and I am sure you will find a lot of things that will interest you."

"So many that I only wish Christmas was further away!" Lavela laughed.

"As it is quite near," the Duke answered, "you will have to work very hard, because I want my first production to be outstanding."

"I will try . . I will really try to be . . good," Lavela promised.

"I am sure you will be," the Duke smiled.

He sat down at the piano and taking off her bonnet as if without it she felt more free Lavela picked up the music.

She sang it through once.

"Please let us do it again," she pleaded.

The Duke was accompanying her softly on the piano when the door was suddenly flung open and Fiona walked in.

The Duke stopped playing.

Fiona was looking even more spectacular than usual.

The gown she wore under a long fur cape was of emerald green which was one of her favourite colours.

There were ostrich feathers to match in her hat, and emeralds glittered in her ears.

She walked across the room to where the piano stood on a low platform.

As the Duke rose slowly to his feet she said:

"Sheldon! How could you leave London without telling me? I could not believe that you had gone home – alone!"

There was a pause before the last word and she looked at Lavela enquiringly.

"I sent you a note informing you that I had many things to see to here," the Duke answered coldly, "and wished for the moment to be alone!"

"Alone!" Fiona exclaimed. "I have never heard of such nonsense! And, darling, you must be aware that I have been counting the days, the hours, the minutes until your return!"

"I shall soon be returning to London," the Duke said. "So your journey here was quite unnecessary."

Before Fiona could reply he went on:

"Let me introduce you to Miss Lavela Ashley, who has a delightful soprano voice and will take part in the Play I have written for the opening of my Theatre, Miss Ashley – Lady Faversham!"

Lavela held out her hand, but Fiona did not move.

She only regarded her with an expression which the Duke was well aware was both contemptuous and disagreeable.

"Why have I never met you before?" Fiona enquired.

"Because I have never been here until today," Lavela replied.

"That is true," the Duke said. "In fact, I discovered Miss Ashley only yesterday, and her father, who is the Vicar of Little Bedlington, is at the moment on a tour of the house."

He thought as he spoke that Fiona relaxed.

He was well aware of what she was thinking.

He would have been quite ready for her to go on doing so if he had not wished to protect Lavela.

He was certain the angel-like girl from the Vicarage had never in her life met anyone like Fiona.

It was obvious from the way she was looking at the older woman that she was surprised, if nothing else, by her appearance.

"Of course, dearest, I could not bear to think of you being here and lonely with no one intelligent to talk to," Fiona said to the Duke in a very different tone of voice. "So I collected just a few friends and we came down as quickly as we could."

"Who is with you?" the Duke asked in an uncompromising voice.

"As I had so little time, I just invited Isobel Henley since her husband is away and Joscelyn, who is very anxious to see you, accompanied us."

"Joscelyn!"

The Duke with difficulty, prevented his voice from ringing out angrily.

The last person he wanted here at this moment was his Cousin.

Then he remembered that Joscelyn might have insisted on coming anyway.

His interest in seeing him had nothing to do with Fiona.

At the same time, he could feel his anger rising.

Then he told himself he would have to tread very carefully.

In the past there would have been nothing unusual and in fact it was expected, in Fiona being with him at Moor Park.

As she had no idea that he had discovered about her, she had considered it almost her duty to follow him.

To see that everything ran smoothly and he was not lonely.

It suddenly struck him that it would be horrifying for

anyone so young and unspoilt as Lavela to discover his association with Fiona.

With a note of authority in his voice he said:

"Order tea for you and your guests in the Blue Room. Miss Ashley and I will join you when we have finished rehearsing."

He spoke so positively that Fiona was wise enough not to argue.

"Of course, Sheldon dear," she replied. "I will do whatever you want. But you have not yet said how pleased you are to see me."

She spoke in her usual flirtatious manner, looking at him with a seductive expression in her eyes.

"It is certainly a surprise," the Duke replied abruptly.

He turned away as he spoke and sat down again at the piano.

Fiona hesitated.

Then as there was nothing else she could do but leave, she swept from the room, shutting the door noisily behind her.

The Duke did not speak.

He merely started to play one of his own compositions which had given him more pleasure than anything else he had ever done.

As he played the music seemed to sweep away his anger.

For a moment he forgot the three people who had come uninvited to his house and was conscious only of Lavela.

He felt her move a little nearer so that she could watch his fingers.

Then as he brought his composition to an end she was completely silent.

He appreciated her silence.

He knew it meant far more than the gushing but superficial praise he would have received from Fiona.

Then Lavela said:

"That was lovely . . absolutely lovely! I am sure you composed it yourself."

"How do you know that?" the Duke asked.

"Because I knew what you were feeling while you played, and the music was . . a part of you."

He was astonished that she should be so perceptive.

After a moment he said:

"I think you understand perhaps better than most people that when there is a melody in your mind, it does not come entirely from the brain."

"No, of course it does not," Lavela agreed. "It comes from one's heart and one's soul. That is what I feel when I am singing."

"I think," the Duke said as if he had just discovered it for himself, "that is what music is all about!"

Chapter Four

As the Duke finished speaking, the door opened and the Vicar came in.

"I have seen a great deal of the house, Your Grace," he said, "and I hear your guests have arrived. I think therefore Lavela and I should now return home."

"There is no hurry," the Duke said quickly. "In fact, I wanted to ask you, now I realise how interested you are in music, if you know anybody who would take the part in my play of an elderly woman?"

He did not wait for the Vicar to reply, but went on:

"Your daughter will be the angel who comes to tell her that, however old she may be, she is still needed, and when finally she dies she will still go on helping those she loves from Heaven."

The Duke became aware that the Vicar was staring at him in astonishment.

Then as if he felt he was being rude he said quickly:

"That sounds exactly what is needed as a Christmas message, Your Grace!"

"Do you think, Papa," Lavela interposed, "that *Madame* would play the part of the old lady?"

The Vicar hesitated and the Duke looking from one to the other asked:

"Are you telling me there is another genius in Little Bedlington?"

"There is, Your Grace, and it would not be hard, if you approached her personally, to persuade Mrs. Grantham to take the part."

"You mean she has a good voice?" the Duke asked.

"She was, before she married an Englishman, Maria Colzaio."

The Duke was still.

"But – do you mean – you cannot mean –!"

"Yes, the famous Maria Colzaio!"

"And she lives in Little Bedlington? I do not believe it! Why was I not told?"

The Vicar smiled.

"Maria Calzaio, who was, as you know, one of the most famous Italian Opera singers in Europe, retired when she was sixty and married James Grantham, an Englishman."

He paused a moment before he went on:

"They were very happy and she was content to know nobody and forget that she had ever been a *Prima Donna*. Then he died."

"When was that?" the Duke enquired.

"Nearly two years ago," the Vicar replied, "and now we have just been able to coax *Madame* into coming to see us occasionally. Six months ago she started to teach Lavela to sing."

"So that accounts for her having such superb intonation," the Duke said, "apart from the fact that her voice is unique."

"That is what I thought myself," the Vicar said simply, "and I am sure, now that *Madame* is interested in life again, that if Your Grace asked her to perform with Lavela she would do so."

72

"I will come to see her tomorrow," the Duke said. "And as I also want to talk over what Lavela has to do, may I come to you tomorrow morning?"

He thought as he spoke that for him to go to the Vicarage would be far better than for Lavela to come again to Moor Park.

If she did Fiona might try to make trouble.

"We shall be delighted to see you!" the Vicar answered. "And of course we hope Your Grace will stay to luncheon."

"Thank you very much," the Duke said, "that is just what I would like to do."

He picked up his music score. Then he said:

"I suppose you have no more talent in Little Bedlington with which to astound me?"

Lavela looked at her father.

"Papa has taught eight men in the Parish to be Bell-Ringers and I promise you, they are very, very good!"

The Duke knew that bell-ringing went back into Mediaeval times.

Then bells, held by the ringers one in each hand, were tuned to the Tonic Sol-Fa.

When they rang them rhythmically they could produce music as well as a piano could.

"Then that completes my programme for the evening!" he said with satisfaction. "It will be unique in that there will be no professionals! An evening when I introduce Little Bedlington to the Social World."

The Vicar laughed.

"I hope we shall not fail you," Lavela said. "You must remember that no one outside the village knows anything about us, except of course 'Madame', as we always call her."

"I doubt if she will want anybody in the audience to know who she is," the Vicar said, "but of course we must leave that to His Grace."

"And you will arrange for me to see her tomorrow?" the Duke asked.

"Of course," the Vicar said, "and we shall be awaiting with pleasure your arrival at eleven o'clock."

The Duke saw them to the door.

As the Vicar drove away in the old-fashioned gig which had a hood over the two front seats he thought he must be dreaming.

How was it possible for all this musical talent to dwell on his Estate and he had never had the slightest idea of it?

The truth was he knew, that he had always been very reticent about how musical he was.

While in London he attended Concerts and Operas when they were performed by well-known artistes, but he usually went alone.

He was now extremely excited that the opening of his Theatre would take exactly the form he wanted.

He would not need professionals who would want to sing what they considered their best pieces and give a performance which might not please his special audience.

He knew that his relations, if nobody else, would be touched by the idea of the village children singing to them.

He knew too that they would be thrilled to learn that Maria Colzaio was there in person.

Then as he turned from the front door to go back into the hall he remembered something he had been able to forget for the moment.

It was that Fiona had to be coped with and also his Cousin Joscelyn.

74

"Lady Faversham and the Countess of Henley, Your Grace, are in the Blue Drawing-Room," Norton the Butler told him.

As he spoke the Duke knew exactly what he must do.

He walked quickly in the opposite direction down a passage which led him to the Estate Office.

It also provided a Secretary's Room and he was sure he would find Mr. Watson there.

He was not mistaken.

Mr. Watson was sitting at one desk and his assistant was at another.

As the Duke entered they both stood up.

"I wish to speak to you alone, Watson," the Duke said.

The assistant immediately left the room.

The Duke sat down at the desk he had vacated and started to write a note on a piece of his crested writing-paper.

"Now listen, Watson," he said as he did so, "I want you to send this immediately to Colonel and Mrs. Robertson. It tells them I have arrived unexpectedly with a party from London, and should be delighted if they would dine with me this evening and stay for the next two nights."

He paused before he added:

"I have suggested it might be dangerous with such a heavy frost for them to drive home late."

Mr. Watson took the note after the Duke had put it into an envelope.

As he did so he asked:

"Who is at the Dower House?"

"You remember, Your Grace, you loaned it to Lord and Lady Bredon while they are having their own house repaired after it was damaged by fire."

"Yes, of course!" the Duke exclaimed.

He started to write another note and Mr. Watson waited.

"I have asked Lady Bredon, who is of course my Cousin, if they will come here for the weekend," the Duke said, "and if she would act as hostess to my party."

He thought as he spoke that Mr. Watson looked surprised, though he made no comment.

Enid Bredon was a rather bossy, overwhelming woman of fifty whom the Duke usually avoided whenever possible.

He had found it difficult to refuse what was almost a demand on her part to be allowed to use the Dower House.

He had however, made no effort until now to include her in any of his house-parties.

He thought now with a slight twist of his lips that if anyone could prevent Fiona from playing hostess it would be Enid Bredon.

He put the note he had finished into Mr. Watson's hands, then said:

"I want a large luncheon-party tomorrow, an even larger dinner-party, and the same applies every day until my present guests leave."

His voice was sharp, but Mr. Watson, with his usual tact, only said quietly:

"I suppose, Your Grace, you wish me to ask all the nearest neighbours?"

"Invite those who live further away, and ask them to stay," the Duke replied. "There is plenty of room in the house, and I am sure you can always get extra help from the village."

"Yes, of course, Your Grace."

Mr. Watson hesitated, then asked somewhat tentatively:

"Are you leaving the choice of Your Grace's guests to me?"

"You know better than I do, Watson, who is available, and I want the house full – do you understand? Until, as I say, Lady Faversham and Mr. Joscelyn leave."

Mr. Watson was well aware there was a reason for this very unusual request.

As the Duke left the office he rang for his assistant and started to put the wheels in motion which nobody could do more efficiently than he could.

There was a cynical smile on the Duke's lips as he walked towards the Blue Room.

He was determined to make things as difficult as possible for Joscelyn to approach him.

He knew he was determined to do so and to plead for money with which to pay his debts.

The Duke also wanted, in what he thought was a very subtle manner, to show Fiona that her reign had ended.

As he entered the Blue Drawing-Room she gave a little cry of delight and ran towards him eagerly.

"Oh, here you are at last, dearest Sheldon!" she exclaimed. "We wondered how you could have immersed yourself so quickly in Parochial matters!"

What she said told the Duke that she had made enquiries as to who Lavela was.

She would have been informed by the servants that the Vicar was also in the house.

The Duke did not answer Fiona, but walked towards the Countess of Henley and kissed her on the cheek.

"I am surprised to see you here, Isobel," he said. "I

always believed you hated the country at this time of the year!"

"Moor Park is not the country!" Isobel Henley replied. "It is a Palace of luxury, and that is different!"

It was the sort of remark that always made people laugh and Joscelyn obliged.

"How are you, Sheldon?" he asked the Duke. "You will understand that as these two lovely ladies wished to follow you, I could only oblige by being their escort."

"Of course!" the Duke replied. "And I hope you will not find your visit too boring."

He then sat down beside Lady Henley and started to talk to her about their mutual friends in London.

She was an acknowledged Beauty.

At the same time she had a sharp tongue which could at times, be venomous.

She was more or less separated from her husband.

He preferred being on his Estate in the North of England, while she enjoyed the endless round of social events in Mayfair.

To the Duke's knowledge she had taken lover after lover.

He knew now as he flirted with her she was considering whether it would be possible to wean him away from Fiona.

He was aware that both Fiona and Joscelyn were watching him.

It was with a sense of relief that as they finished tea the Butler came to his side to say:

"Mr. Watson would like a word with you, Your Grace!"

"Forgive me," the Duke said.

He rose to his feet. Then looking down at Isobel he remarked:

"You are more amusing than ever, Isobel, and I am looking forward to dinner tonight!"

The Countess gave him a provocative glance.

He was aware as he walked across the room that Fiona was looking after him angrily.

In the hall Mr. Watson was waiting for him.

"I have a reply from Colonel and Mrs. Robertson, Your Grace, who will be arriving in time for dinner. And Lord and Lady Bredon have asked for a carriage to be sent for them immediately!"

"Thank you, Watson!" the Duke said, "and I want the Countess of Henley on my right at dinner and Mrs. Robertson on my left."

Mr. Watson made a note on the pad he was carrying.

"Lady Bredon will sit at the other end of the table tonight and for the rest of her visit," the Duke ordered.

He then walked quickly in the direction of his Study.

When he got there he locked himself in and started to work on the Programme for his Opening Night.

It was incredible to think that he had Maria Colzaio living on his doorstep.

As he thought of it, he realised that Little Bedlington was actually by road nearly six miles from Moor Park.

It would be dangerous for the Robertsons to drive home at night when they lived on the other side of the Park.

It would certainly be very dangerous for the children to return to the village on Saturday after the performance.

"They too must stay the night," he decided.

He thought it would be amusing and would certainly give everybody something to talk about.

He imagined that many of the children were quite small.

This would mean he would have to accommodate at least some of their mothers to look after them.

He made notes of everything he decided upon.

He would give them to Mr. Watson after he had finished arranging the house-party.

The Duke felt he was almost like a General, working out a campaign against the enemy which, in this case, consisted of just two people.

However, both in their own way were extremely formidable.

Fiona and Joscelyn joined the Duke in the Drawing-Room where they assembled before dinner.

It was obvious that they were astounded to find Lord and Lady Bredon there.

Colonel and Mrs. Robertson were announced a few minutes later.

The newcomers were obviously delighted to have been invited, even at such short notice.

"Surely you have come home very unexpectedly?" Lady Bredon said questioningly.

"When I came back from Holland," the Duke replied, "I was so tired of pompous speeches and long-winded Statesmen that I ran away!"

Everybody laughed at this, and Lord Bredon said:

"I know exactly what you mean, Sheldon, and if the frost ceases you will be much happier hunting."

"It is such a pity you were not here last week," Mrs. Robertson said as they sat down to dinner.

She was delighted to find herself on the Duke's left.

She went into a long and graphic description of last week's runs and a fox they lost.

She added a few criticisms of the huntsmen which the Duke expected.

He usually found her rather a bore.

But tonight he was determined to make a fuss of everyone with the exception of Fiona.

The Countess certainly made the most of her opportunity of sitting on the Duke's right.

She flirted with him and made him laugh.

She managed at the same time to hold Lord Bredon who was on her right, spellbound.

The dinner was excellent.

The Duke thought that with the exception of Fiona, who was looking sulky, everybody enjoyed themselves. When they moved into the Drawing-Room there were two card-tables set out for Whist.

As they were exactly the right number the Duke seated everyone, making sure that his table included neither Fiona nor Joscelyn.

Fiona made every possible attempt to get close to him.

Somehow he managed to be so evasive that she failed.

Finally, while the rest of the party were saying goodnight, she went upstairs to bed.

She gave a lingering look in the Duke's direction which told him exactly what she expected.

The rest of the party stayed talking until Mrs. Robertson said:

"I feel we are being selfish, for I am sure dear Duke, that having come all that way from Holland, you are very tired."

"I am rather," the Duke admitted.

His eyes focused on Joscelyn who was moving towards the door.

Rather reluctantly the Countess was following.

Mrs. Robertson finished the lemonade that remained in her glass.

As she did so she said to the Duke:

"What a lovely party! It was so kind of you to have us."

"I was delighted to have you," the Duke replied.

"I have always admired Lady Faversham," Mrs. Robertson went on, "and she is more beautiful than ever."

"I agree with you!" the Duke murmured.

"It is, of course, very sad that she is unable to have a child."

The Duke was still.

"Why do you say that?" he enquired.

"I thought you knew!" Mrs. Robertson said. "My family were near neighbours to the Duke of Cumbria's Estate and I remember Fiona as a child."

"I had no idea of that," the Duke remarked.

"She was fifteen," Mrs. Robertson continued, "when she had an accident out hunting, and it was a very bad one!"

The Duke was listening intently as Mrs. Robertson went on:

"She eventually recovered, but the doctors said she could never have a child, and I have often thought that was why her marriage to Eric Faversham broke up."

She gave a short laugh.

"I know of course that he was a 'naughty boy' in many ways, but I feel if there had been a son it might have made all the difference to their marriage."

She finished speaking and started to walk towards the door.

The Duke followed her, feeling as if he had been shocked into silence.

It had never struck him for one moment when he had

considered marrying Fiona that she might be unable to provide him with an heir.

He knew now it would have been disastrous if he had asked her to marry him, and found this out later.

He thought he must have been very stupid.

Why had he not asked why during the years she was married to Eric Faversham, who was, if nothing else, an ardent lover, they had never had any children.

He said goodnight to Mrs. Robertson at the door of her bedroom and moved on to his own.

It was at the far end of the corridor.

As he did so he thought that by the grace of God he had been saved.

It was from something so disastrous that it did not bear thinking about.

Of course Fiona in her desire to be the Duchess of Moorminster would not have told him.

He had a suspicion however, that Joscelyn knew the truth.

It would certainly be greatly to his advantage in his desire to be the next Duke if the Duchess was unable to produce an heir.

As the Duke went to his room he felt as if Lavela was telling him that he must say a prayer of gratitude.

He had been saved from asking Fiona to be his wife as he had seriously considered doing when he came back from Holland.

His Valet was waiting for him, and when the man left him he knew he had another problem in front of him.

One which he had little time to solve.

Fiona would be waiting for him.

She would find it very strange and would undoubtedly be suspicious if he did not join her.

He had no intention of doing this.

At the same time, he knew she would not hesitate to come to his room when she realised he was not coming to hers.

The obvious answer was to lock his door.

But it struck him that she might knock on it, and there was always the chance that she might be heard doing so.

It was certainly something the Robertsons would talk about, and so would the Bredons.

With a swiftness of thought which had got him out of many political difficulties, the Duke made up his mind.

He disliked his house to be cold.

He had therefore given orders that in the Winter a fire was to be lit in every room, whether they were in use or not.

There were two men whose duty it was to go round the great house making up the fires.

This occupied them from first thing in the morning until last thing at night.

The Duke therefore merely moved a little further down the corridor to a room that was not occupied.

The fire there was nevertheless burning brightly.

Once inside he locked the door and got into the bed.

In the morning he would tell his Valet that the fire in his room was smoking, and he had therefore moved into another room.

Before he fell asleep he had forgotten about Fiona.

He was once again thinking of his theatre and Lavela's voice.

He also had another idea about how the whole Programme should start which he wanted to discuss with the Vicar.

As he fell asleep another tune came to his mind.

This time for the Overture which would be played as soon as the audience was seated.

The following morning the Duke had left the house before Fiona and Isobel Henley came downstairs.

The Robertsons and the Bredons had breakfast at nine o'clock.

Mr. Watson in the Duke's absence asked them what they wished to do.

They replied they would like to go riding.

Only Lady Bredon said she had some letters to write.

Later, perhaps this afternoon, she added, she would like a carriage in which she could call on some of her friends.

When the rest of the party had set out on their ride, Mr. Watson on the Duke's orders showed her his list.

It contained the names of those who were arriving for luncheon and also for dinner.

Most of them had accepted the Duke's invitation to stay in the house.

"Whatever made the Duke suddenly decide to entertain in this wholesale fashion?" Lady Bredon asked with her usual blunt frankness.

"I gather His Grace was very bored while he was in Holland, My Lady," Watson replied, "and a number of these guests have in fact, not been invited to Moor Park for a long time."

"If I have told Sheldon once, I have told him a thousand times," Lady Bredon said, "that he should give a Garden Party in the Summer as his father did, and get all the bores off at the same time!"

"I am sure that is a good idea, My Lady," Mr. Watson agreed.

"What is more," Lady Bredon went on, "he should have a series of evening parties such as we will have tonight."

She paused a moment to smile as she said;

"I know the 'Locals' will greatly enjoy mixing with my Cousin's smart London friends."

Mr. Watson declined tactfully to say the obvious.

Which was that the Duke's London friends would not much care for the "Locals".

Instead he informed Lady Bredon that he would bring her all the other acceptances as they arrived.

He also gave her the task of placing the guests at meals.

It was the Duke of course who had told him exactly what to do.

He had then ridden away towards Little Bedlington, like a boy playing truant from School.

He actually arrived at the Vicarage before eleven o'clock, but Lavela was there ready to greet him.

"You have really come!" she said. "When I told Mama what you were planning, she thought we were joking."

"I must assure your mother that I am very serious," the Duke replied, as he walked into the Vicarage.

He was surprised, although of course he did not say so, at how well-furnished it was.

It was obvious that the Vicar had extremely good taste.

The curtains and carpets were attractive and there were some pictures which the Duke would have liked to own himself.

He knew who was responsible however.

After he had worked with the Vicar and Lavela on the Programme he met Mrs. Ashley.

First, however, they had to concentrate on his determination to produce the whole Programme entirely from Little Bedlington.

Of course a great deal depended on whether Maria Colzaio would consent to perform.

The Vicar was optimistic, and he had arranged to take the Duke to meet her after luncheon.

The Duke sat down at the very good grand-piano which stood in the Drawing-Room of the Vicarage and started to play.

"What is that?" the Vicar asked.

"It is the Overture," he explained. "I intend it shall be played on two pianos – one played by Lavela and one by myself."

"That is wonderful!" Lavela exclaimed. "But . . supposing I am not . . good enough?"

"That is a question I should be asking of myself!" the Duke replied.

She laughed.

"Now I think you are being modest! You play exceptionally well, while I am only a beginner!"

"I am not listening to that nonsense!" the Duke asserted. "You will play with me, and I already have an idea for a new composition which will delight everybody!"

"I must have time to practise it," Lavela said breathlessly.

"I promise I will finish it tonight," the Duke answered.

"Then what happens?" the Vicar enquired.

"You appear before the curtains," the Duke explained, "to wish the audience a happy evening and tell them in verse what they are going to see."

He smiled before he added;

"I imagine, after what you have told me of your performances in the past, you have a Fancy-Dress somewhere which might be appropriate."

"I can either be a Harlequin or a Courtier at the time of Charles II," the Vicar replied, "complete with wig and moustache!"

The Duke laughed.

"I leave the choice to you!"

"What happens then?" Lavela asked excitedly.

"The curtain will go up," the Duke answered, "and your choir will sing exactly as I heard them in the Church."

"Just the choir?"

"You will conduct them from the pit so that no one sees you clearly. On the stage it will just be the children."

Lavela nodded and the Duke went on;

"I think you will have to include some of my nephews and nieces who will be with me at Christmas. They will be disappointed if they are not allowed to play some small part in the performance."

"Of course," Lavela agreed, "and if I can, I would like to have at least one rehearsal with them."

"I may send them here to you," the Duke said, "but I have a new plan for the actual night of the performance."

He then explained how he thought it would be a good idea for the children and their mothers to stay the night at Moor Park.

Lavela clapped her hands together.

"It is the most wonderful idea I have ever heard!" she said. "They will be so thrilled, so excited! But are you sure there will be enough room for them?"

The Duke laughed.

"They will have the whole of the East Wing, which has over twenty bedrooms in it!"

"I apologise," Lavela said. "I had forgotten how enormous your house is!"

"I can imagine nothing that would please the Parish more," the Vicar said, "and it is very generous of you, Your Grace!"

"I am being entirely selfish," the Duke replied. "You know as well as I do that it is Lavela and Maria Colzaio, if she accepts, who will make it the most sensational evening that has ever been known in my house!"

"I shall feel .. terrible if .. you are .. disappointed," Lavela answered.

She looked so worried as she spoke that the Duke said quickly;

"I have a feeling none of us will be disappointed, and we will enjoy the evening as much as the children will."

"I hope you are .. right," Lavela said in a low voice.

"After that," the Duke went on, "there will be the Bell-Ringers. I only ask you, Vicar, to make quite certain that they play happy, really 'Christmassy' tunes that even the most tone-deaf member of the audience can recognise."

The Vicar laughed.

"What you are saying, Your Grace, is that they are not to be too 'high-brow'."

"Exactly!"

"They will certainly do their best," the Vicar smiled. "And I need not tell you how thrilled the performers will be!"

"What comes after that?" Lavela asked as if she could not prevent herself from hurrying on to her entrance.

"Then it is your time," he answered, "and I just need two girls, one to give the flowers to Maria Colzaio, the other to beg from her advice regarding her love-affair."

"I think I have the right one for that," Lavela said. "The Doctor's daughter is seventeen and a very intelligent girl. Papa and I both think she will play the part to perfection."

"I am sure she will," the Vicar said. "She has already been a 'shining light' in our Nativity Play that takes place every Christmas, and was a very successful Juliet when our School put on *Romeo and Juliet* a few months ago."

The Duke did not say anything.

He could think of no other village on his Estate which would have its children performing Shakespeare.

"What happens after that?" the Vicar enquired.

"I was going to ask Lavela if the children knew any other Carols which they can sing as well as they sing *It Came Upon the Midnight Clear*."

"Yes of course they know several," Lavela replied. "But I think the best is *O Little Town of Bethlehem*."

"Splendid!" the Duke exclaimed. "They can sing that and again you can conduct them from the Pit. Then 'Father Christmas' which is me, will arrive on a sleigh which will be pulled into place by four of my footmen."

He paused before he went on;

"The sleigh will be loaded with presents for everybody in the audience. I will hand the presents to the children who will run down from the stage and present them to everybody in the Stalls."

He looked at the Vicar as he went on;

"While they are doing that, I want a Male Voice Choir, which I have a feeling you have somewhere in Little Bedlington, to sing the Carols which everybody knows."

Lavela laughed.

"How did you know Papa had a Male Voice Choir?" she asked.

"You told me your father had a good voice," the Duke answered, "and I could not believe that he would be the only man singing in his Church."

The Vicar laughed.

"Your Grace's quite right! We have six men who really sing extremely well. We entertain not only those who come to Church, but also go to the local Inn to herald in the New Year."

The Duke threw up his hands.

"I only find it extraordinary that you have 'hidden your light under a bushel' for so long! But now the whole Estate will be aware that Little Bedlington is an example to every other village."

"I shall be very unpopular," the Vicar said ruefully.

"Does it matter?" the Duke asked. "And perhaps I will set an example and a challenge to other Landlords to encourage musical talent on their estates."

"That is certainly a very good idea," the Vicar answered, "and it may result in more people going to Church."

The Duke had no wish to discuss this.

His Church was just inside the Park.

Yet when he had a sophisticated week-end house-party he often missed attending Matins on Sunday.

"One thing is quite certain," Lavela said. "We must start work at once and I will tell the children when they come to Church after School this afternoon that they are going to perform at Moor Park and stay the night there."

"I do not think you will have any absentees after that!" the Vicar smiled.

91

The Duke then sat down at the piano to play to Lavela his Overture.

When he had done so she took his seat at the piano and played it with just one hesitation, brilliantly.

"We shall have to practise this with two pianos," the Duke said. "I do not suppose you have another one here?"

"I am afraid not," Lavela replied.

The Vicar had left the room.

The Duke knew that she hoped he would ask her to Moor Park, so that she could play there in his beautiful Music Room.

He was, however, still uncertain, as to how much trouble Fiona might make and was determined to be out of the house as much as possible.

"I will send a piano over tomorrow," he said, "which will be an upright one. I will have to arrange for the two Grand Pianos we shall require for our duet to be fitted somehow on the stage."

"There is not room for them in the Pit?" Lavela asked.

He shook his head.

"No, we have an upright one there."

"I understand," Lavela said.

"I would like to come here while we are rehearsing," the Duke went on, "for the simple reason that my house is now full of guests. I do not want them to hear any of the music until the Opening Night of the Theatre."

"No, of course not," Lavela agreed, "and I know Mama and Papa will be delighted for you to come here whenever you wish."

Both the Vicar and his wife echoed this.

Mrs. Ashley had appeared just before luncheon and it

was no surprise to the Duke to find that she was very beautiful.

But, he thought, she was not English.

She spoke perfect English, but there was just something about her which made him sure she had some other nationality.

However, he realised that, if she was not shy, she was very retiring.

While she was extremely pleasant and hospitable during luncheon she disappeared immediately afterwards.

Because she was so beautiful and the Vicar was so handsome, it was not surprising that their only child was lovely.

But it did not account for Lavela's angelic looks.

Except, the Duke thought, that the Vicar and his wife were very much in love with each other.

He was too experienced not to be aware of the softness in their voices when they spoke to each other and the expression in their eyes.

It seemed to him almost extraordinary after they had been married for so many years.

But he knew it was very much the same as the love that had existed between his father and mother.

Unless they were together they had always appeared unhappy and restless.

When they were together the way they looked at each other and the way they spoke made it clear to the most obtuse outsider that they were still in love.

"That is what I want too," the Duke thought.

He knew however, that because he was a Duke he was very unlikely to be married for himself alone.

He would be deceived, as he had been by Fiona, over and over again.

It was a depressing thought.

He pushed it aside, concentrating instead on the surprisingly intelligent conversation.

The food was delicious.

He found he was eating dishes that were so imaginative that they might have been provided by his very expensive Chef.

When luncheon was over he said to Mrs. Ashley;

"I hope you will not think me impertinent when I say how very much I have enjoyed your delicious and unusual meal!"

He smiled beguilingly as he said;

"As a traveller, I have always known that the French have the best *cuisine* in the world, and the English are perfectly content with what is simple and obvious."

The Vicar laughed.

"That is certainly true, Your Grace, but I should explain that I have travelled a great deal abroad and have become a *gourmet*. I believe that my wife could, if she wished, open a Restaurant and make an outstanding success of it!"

The Duke raised his eye-brows.

"Is your husband telling me that you cooked this meal?" he asked Mrs. Ashley.

"Some of it," Mrs. Ashley replied. "But I have also taught two women from the village who look after us extremely well how to produce the dishes which are my husband's favourites, and to be prepared to try those I appreciate."

"I really cannot bear it!" the Duke exclaimed. "If you astound me with any more of your brilliant talents in Little Bedlington I shall leave Moor Park and come to live here amongst you!"

"You are very welcome to do so," the Vicar replied, "although I think you would find it rather cramped!"

"But how romantic it would be," Lavela exclaimed, "to have a Duke living in one of our cottages!"

"I am afraid what would happen then is that hundreds of people would follow me, and it would change from being a charming village into an ugly Town," the Duke replied.

They were all thinking this was an amusing idea and laughing about it when Mrs. Ashley disappeared.

It was then the Vicar said it was time to go and visit Maria Colzaio.

As they drove away in the Duke's carriage he was thinking he had never enjoyed a meal more.

He felt certain his collection of guests at Moor Park would not have found their luncheon so stimulating and entertaining.

As the horses increased their pace the Duke sitting beside the Vicar said;

"You must be aware, Vicar, that I am extremely curious as to why, seeing how beautiful your wife and daughter are, you bury yourselves in the country!"

There was a perceptible pause.

The Duke realised he had intruded on something intimate.

After what seemed a long silence the Vicar replied;

"There are reasons why we should do so, Your Grace, and I am sure you will understand that they are very personal ones. We are extremely happy just as we are, and it is something I do not wish to discuss."

"Of course, and I apologise if I have intruded," the Duke said quickly.

"There is no need," the Vicar said, "and I am in fact

delighted that Lavela has found something as exciting as your Theatre to occupy her and where her voice will be heard by discriminating people."

He paused before he went on;

"What is perfect for my wife and myself might become in time frustrating for a young girl."

"I understand," the Duke said, "and I promise you, Vicar, I will make sure that Lavela enjoys herself; at any rate this Christmas."

"Thank you," the Vicar said.

They drove on.

The Duke was aware there was nothing more he could say.

He was however, no less intensely curious.

He was determined to try somehow to discover, without causing any embarrassment, the truth.

Chapter Five

In the next few days the Duke thought he had been very clever.

He left the house early each morning to go riding.

Then he either rode to Little Bedlington or else drove there in his Chaise.

He had of course persuaded Maria Colzaio to sing for him.

She had offered him her Drawing-Room in which to rehearse with her and Lavela undisturbed and in comfort.

It was a beautiful room containing a magnificent grand-piano which the Duke enjoyed playing.

As the Vicar had said, Maria Colzaio's voice was not as high as it had been.

But it still had the beautiful warm quality that had made her so famous.

After the first day when she was obviously a little nervous, she said to the Duke;

"I am really enjoying myself, and may I say, Your Grace, it is wonderful to have an accompanist who plays as well as you."

"I think this is one of the most exciting things I have ever done," the Duke replied, "and to hear you sing one of my own compositions is beyond my wildest dreams!"

In contrast, Lavela's young, clear voice, was, he thought, very moving.

He knew that when she performed before the audience including the Prince and Princess of Wales, they would be astonished.

He had deliberately not told the Ashleys, nor Maria Colzaio who his principal guests would be.

He thought it would make Lavela nervous.

He was afraid too it might upset Maria Colzaio who still wished to be incognito.

He therefore merely told her they were performing for his Christmas Party guests.

Also for the mothers of the children who were perform - ing who could be squeezed into the back of the Stalls.

There were in fact only five who were going to stay the night at Moor Park.

The rest could not leave their other children, who were still small.

"You have no idea what excitement you have caused!" Lavela told him. "If you had thrown a bomb into the centre of the village it could not have been more sensational!"

When she was not rehearsing, Lavela was finding the right clothes for the children to wear.

While they sang their Carols they would wear their own best dresses.

But she decided they should wear also a small wreath of mistletoe which they made themselves.

It would be tied at the back of their heads with red ribbons.

They would also hold a little bouquet of mistletoe and holly.

"I wish I had not thought of that," she complained to the Duke. "I have been removing the thorns from the holly and my fingers are very sore!"

"I have always believed that angels fear no pain!" he teased.

"Then I must have come from somewhere very different from Heaven!" Lavela retorted.

They found so many things to laugh about at the rehearsals with Maria Colzaio.

It sent the Duke away so cheerful that he began to forget the difficulties at Moor Park.

The first night he knew from the condition of his bed when he returned to his room that Fiona had waited for him.

After that he locked his door.

He had also moved Fiona and Isobel Henley from the corridor in which his own room was situated.

He told Mr. Watson what he was to do.

When they returned from a drive the second afternoon of their visit, Mr. Watson informed them very apologetically that he had been obliged to change their rooms.

"What do you mean by that?" Fiona asked sharply.

"Two of His Grace's relatives are arriving tomorrow, My Lady," Mr. Watson replied.

"What has that to do with me and *my* room?" Fiona demanded.

"*Your* room, as you call it, My Lady," Mr. Watson replied, "has always been used by His Grace's grandmother the Dowager Duchess, and Lady Henley's by His Grace's Aunt the Marchioness of Seaford."

There was nothing either of the uninvited visitors could say to this.

Fiona, of course, was furious.

She was already very angry because she had found it impossible ever to speak to the Duke alone.

He had always left the house before she came downstairs in the morning.

To her astonishment, he never returned for luncheon, although a number of other guests had arrived.

Lady Bredon was the hostess, and there was nothing Fiona could do to assert her authority.

When the Duke came down to dinner on his return from Little Bedlington he made certain that the Drawing-Room was half-full before he appeared.

He apologised profusely for being late, explaining that he was working on his plans for Christmas.

He did not wish too many outsiders to be present at the Opening of the Theatre.

He was therefore careful not to mention what was to happen.

"I have to see you alone," Fiona hissed at him, as the gentlemen joined the ladies and the party was bigger than ever.

"Of course!" the Duke agreed pleasantly. "But I cannot think when."

Fiona drew in her breath.

She was just about to give him the obvious answer when the Duke moved away.

He was busy arranging his guests at the card-tables.

The younger members of the party were dancing to an Orchestra in what was known as the "Small Ball-Room".

The Duke watched them swinging round to a spirited Waltz.

He suddenly thought it was something Lavela would have enjoyed.

"I should have invited her," he thought.

100

He had not done so simply because he did not want to spoil the impact she would make when she appeared as an angel in the Theatre.

Now he thought he had been very selfish.

He remembered he had promised her father that she should be entertained.

On Christmas Day the Duke knew that Lavela would be busy playing the organ in her father's Church.

It was traditional for him to sit in the family pew in his own Church.

He read one of the lessons, and listened to a Sermon from the Vicar who was also his Private Chaplain.

This he had requested to be short and to last no longer than ten minutes.

When the party returned to Moor Park they filled the great table in the centre of the Banqueting Hall.

There were also two smaller tables at which Lady Bredon had placed the younger members of the family.

There was turkey and Christmas pudding which was carried in by the Chef having first had brandy poured over it and lit.

And of course there were crackers and plenty of champagne with which to drink the Duke's health.

He made a short speech, paying a tribute to his grandmother.

He spoke too of some of his older relatives who were delighted by the attention.

Afterwards the gentlemen sat for a long time drinking port or brandy and exchanging jokes.

As was traditional, in the evening the Duke received his tenants and employees in the huge Servants' Hall.

His grandmother received them, and his nieces and

nephews handed out Christmas presents to everybody present.

It was a custom that had been started by the Duke's Great-Grandfather and had been a tradition in the family ever since.

Then the local Carol Singers from the village sang in the Servants' Hall.

In the Duke's opinion they did not even begin to sing as well as the children of Little Bedlington.

After that most people were tired.

So there were no further festivities on Christmas night.

He also had had a rehearsal with the Male Choir which had been trained by Mr. Ashley.

They were to be appropriately dressed when they appeared in the *Finale* on Saturday.

A number of costumes had been found in Little Bedlington, but the Duke also scoured his attics.

He went to the house Seamstress with Mr. Watson to see what else was required.

Early on the morning of Boxing Day he arrived at the Vicarage bringing with him his Christmas Presents.

He had chosen a very special one for Lavela.

He was sure it was something she would appreciate.

It was a snuff-box which he had seen in one of the shops in Bond Street.

He wondered at the time to whom he should give it.

Fiona would not appreciate anything that was not jewellery with which to bedeck herself.

The snuff-box was enamelled with a painting in the centre of small cupids holding a wreath of roses.

It was exquisitely done and round the picture were small diamonds interspersed with pearls.

When Lavela opened the Duke's present she stared as if she could not believe what she was seeing.

Then she asked;

"This is . . for . . me?"

"I thought when you admired my collection that you might like to start your own 'Aladdin's Cave," the Duke replied.

For a moment she was silent.

Then she said in a rapt little voice which told him how thrilled she was:

"How can I thank you . . or find the . . words to tell you that this is the most beautiful thing I have ever seen, let alone possessed!"

"I hoped it would please you," the Duke answered, "and it is also to thank you for singing my compositions so beautifully!"

Because he had had so many meals at the Vicarage he had brought the Vicar a pâté made by his own Chef.

There was also a jar of caviar and a case of champagne.

"I have not enjoyed caviar since I was in Russia!" the Vicar exclaimed.

"You have been to Russia?" the Duke asked in surprise.

"I visited it many years ago," the Vicar replied, "and came back via the Scandinavian countries."

As he spoke he exchanged a glance with his wife which the Duke did not miss.

It was, he thought, obviously part of the puzzle he was hoping to solve.

He had not questioned the Vicar since the first time.

Nevertheless he was still intensely curious.

He longed to know why anyone so intelligent and in

Mrs. Ashley's case, so beautiful, should bury themselves in Little Bedlington.

There was no doubt they were happy.

In fact, he had never seen two people so happy just to be together.

He was determined to bring Lavela in contact with more exciting society than the villagers and the children she taught to sing.

They had all enthused over their presents.

Mrs. Ashley was delighted with the very elegant sunshade he had given her.

Then the Duke said;

"Now that your main Christmas festivities are over, I would like you all to come to Moor Park this evening and stay until next Sunday."

The Vicar looked at him in surprise and the Duke went on:

"I have many young relatives staying with me whom I would like Lavela to meet. Also I think it important now to rehearse in the Theatre itself. As you know, Vicar, a Drawing-Room however large is not the same as a stage."

"You are quite right," the Vicar agreed, "and I see Your Grace's point. At the same time . . "

"Oh, please, Papa," Lavela broke in, "do let us go! I have been wondering how I could suggest that we should have a rehearsal on the stage before the performance. It would be awful if we made a mess of it on the night."

"That is true," the Vicar agreed.

He looked questioningly at his wife who said:

"Of course it is a good idea, Andrew, and I think you and Lavela should go. But I will stay here and only come to Moor Park on Saturday night."

"Is that what you really want?" the Vicar asked in a low voice.

His wife nodded and he said:

"Very well, I will go with Lavela, but I shall have to return on Friday for my service."

"My horses, Vicar, are at your disposal," the Duke said hastily, "and I will of course, send a carriage for Mrs. Ashley early on Saturday evening."

It was all arranged.

When Maria Colzaio – it was impossible to think of her by any other name – said she would come with Mrs. Ashley, the Duke did not make any objections.

He knew they could rehearse quite well without her.

She undoubtedly would be more at home on the stage than anybody else.

So he hurried back to Moor Park to join the Boxing-Day Shoot which was another long-standing family tradition.

His friends were astonished that he should have missed the first two drives, but he was there now for the third.

After luncheon there were two more drives at which the Duke shot brilliantly.

It annoyed him that he had had to alter the position of the guns.

Joscelyn had made no offer to leave Moor Park and had insisted that he should join the Shoot.

The Duke knew in a way it was his own fault that Joscelyn was still there.

His cousin had tried to get him alone, but he had always managed to avoid him at the last moment.

The Duke had the feeling that Joscelyn and Fiona were plotting something, although he had no idea what it might be.

Without appearing to do so, he had noticed that on

several occasions they were whispering together in a conspiratorial manner.

He was quite certain that anything they were saying about him would be derogatory.

At the same time, they were both frantic to succeed in getting him to themselves.

Christmas Day had been difficult when he had been in the house all day.

Now that everybody was thinking about the Shoot, it was easier for him to avoid them.

He had hoped against hope that Fiona would lose her temper and leave before the Prince and Princess of Wales arrived.

But she was made of sterner stuff than to give in so easily.

One moment on Christmas Day had been very revealing.

After luncheon the Duke had joined the ladies in the Drawing-Room for a short time.

He had gone first to his grandmother who was seated by the fireside.

"I hope you are enjoying yourself, Grandmama," he said.

He bent to kiss her.

"It is the best Christmas I have ever known!" the Dowager Duchess replied. "But there is one toast I would have liked to add to those we have just drunk in the Dining-Room."

"What is that?" the Duke answered.

"One to your son and heir, dearest boy," the Duchess replied.

The Duke was wondering what he should answer when he realised that Fiona was standing beside him.

106

For a moment he met her eyes.

As he did so he suddenly was sure she knew he was aware that she was unable to have a child.

Because they had been so close to each other for so long he knew what she was thinking.

She also could read his thoughts.

For a moment they just stared at each other.

Then the Duke bent and kissed his grandmother's cheek and walked out of the room.

When the day's shooting was over, the Duke was congratulated by everybody taking part.

It had been an excellent day's sport.

After tea most of the party retired to rest before dinner.

The Duke however went to the Music Room with Lavela who had just arrived.

Without her being aware of it he locked the door so that they would not be disturbed.

They went over the alterations he had made to the score while they had been rehearsing with Maria Colzaio.

"It is perfect," Lavela exclaimed when they had finished, "completely perfect! If you do any more it will be like over-painting a picture."

"I suppose like all Composers," the Duke said, "I want to achieve perfection."

"And that is what you have done!" Lavela answered.

"Now we must go to dress for dinner," the Duke said. "We are having a dance tonight as I do not want you to be tired tomorrow before the Christening of my Theatre."

"That is what it is going to be?" Lavela asked. "Have you thought of a special name for it?"

"To name it had not occurred to me until this moment,"

the Duke said, "but of course we must choose one!"

They walked up the stairs side by side.

Lavela thought of one name, the Duke another, but they neither of them seemed right.

The Duke escorted her to the room she was to occupy, with her father next door.

There were two people at the end of the corridor talking together.

He realised they were Fiona and Joscelyn.

It flashed through his mind that perhaps, as she had done before, Fiona was consoling herself with Joscelyn.

Then because he was with Lavela and she had an aura of purity about her, he did not want to think of Fiona.

Besides the young people staying in the house, Mr. Watson on the Duke's instructions had invited a number of others in the County to the dance

An Orchestra had been engaged from London.

The Big Ball-Room was opened and decorated with flowers from the hot-houses.

It was something which had often happened before at Moor Park.

But the Duke knew it was the first time for Lavela, and that she had never been to a real Ball.

She was very simply dressed.

Yet once again he thought the white gown which revealed the curves of her breasts and the smallness of her waist was a perfect frame for her beauty.

"That is how she must look when she is the Angel!" he told himself.

The idea pleased him.

While she was far down the table from where he was sitting at dinner, he found himself watching her.

Her eyes were shining.

She was continually laughing at what the two young men on either side of her were saying.

Fiona, he noticed, was also animated but in a very different way.

He was certain that every remark she made had a double meaning.

Every look she gave the men next to her and every movement she made had something seductive about it.

It struck him for the first time that apart from everything else that he now knew about her, she did not really fit in at Moor Park.

He told himself it was something he should have been aware of before.

The men did not linger over their port as they had the previous evening.

The Duke knew the girls, and especially Lavela, were waiting excitedly for partners.

She certainly did not lack them.

The Duke asked her to dance after he had done his duty with the older members of the party.

He thought as he did so that nobody could look more radiant.

"I can see you are enjoying yourself," he remarked.

"I have wings on my feet!" Lavela answered. "This is not an 'Aladdin's Cave' but the Prince's Palace and I am only afraid that when midnight strikes it will all vanish!"

"I shall be very upset if it does!" the Duke smiled. "And I hope if you are handing out roles in your Fairy Story I am Prince Charming!"

"But of course," she answered, "except that you are a Magician at the same time!"

109

The Duke laughed.

"As long as I am not the Demon King I am quite content."

As he spoke Joscelyn passed by.

He thought that if ever there was a candidate suitable for that role, it was his Cousin.

He only hoped that Lavela would never come in contact with anyone so evil.

At the same time, he realised she was being a great success.

The other men in the party were begging her for dances.

When her card was full they insisted that she added a number of extras to it.

The Duke was also aware that the Vicar was enjoying himself.

He was talking to his grandmother and a number of his older relations.

Several of them told the Duke what a delightful man he was and asked why they had not met him before.

"I was very remiss in not knowing he existed," the Duke explained, "and it is something I assure you will be rectified in the future."

"His daughter is lovely!" one of his Aunts said. "I am sure she would be a huge sensation in London."

"It might spoil her," the Duke replied quickly.

When the evening came to an end and the Orchestra played "*God Save The Queen*" everyone regretted it was over.

Those who were going back to their own houses in the County begged the Duke to give another Ball as soon as possible.

"I will certainly think about it," he promised.

When Lavela said goodnight to him she said;

"Thank you for the most exciting evening I have ever had! There is no words by which to describe it except wonderful! I seem to be saying that over and over again ever since I met you."

"All you and I have to concentrate on now," the Duke replied, "is to ensure that everyone will be saying the same on Saturday evening."

"I am quite certain they will say it a thousand times!" Lavela replied.

She walked up the stairs with her father.

The Duke said goodnight to some of his relations, many of the older ones having retired earlier.

Fiona was not to be seen.

That, he thought, was a relief.

Having told Newman the Butler that everything had gone exactly as he had wished he too went up to bed.

He thought as he reached his room where his Valet was waiting that he was not really tired.

It had been a very satisfactory day.

Nothing the Duke thought, could have given him more pleasure than to see Lavela's eyes shining like stars.

He pulled back the curtains to look up at the sky.

As he did so his Valet said;

"Goodnight, Your Grace! Shall I call Your Grace at your usual time?"

"Yes, of course," the Duke answered.

He did not turn round but stayed looking up at the stars.

Then the door opened again and he thought it was irritating that Jenkins had forgotten something.

But when the voice behind him spoke he turned round sharply.

It was not Jenkins who was standing inside his bedroom but his Cousin Joscelyn.

Like the Duke, Lavela when she reached her room was not tired.

Although it was two o'clock in the morning she felt she could have gone on dancing until it was dawn.

She had never danced with a young man before, but she had danced with her father.

Her mother had insisted when she was a child that twice a week she had dancing lessons.

When she had danced with the Duke, it was something, she thought, she would always remember.

It had been easy to follow his steps.

She thought when he held her hand it was as if he transferred some of his strength and brilliance to her.

"He is so wonderful!" she thought, "so very, very wonderful! I cannot believe there is another man like him in the whole world!"

She wanted to thank God for the evening.

In fact, for all the exciting things that had happened to her since the Duke had heard her playing the Church organ.

At home, whenever she wanted to say a special prayer, she could go into the Church by an underground passage.

It had been built many years ago by a Vicar who suffered from a weak chest.

He had not dared to go outside on a cold or windy day.

Now Lavela wished that she could go into the Church and pray in front of the altar.

Then she remembered there was a Chapel at Moor Park.

Her father had told her how beautiful it was.

She had in fact, found out that it was at the back of the house, not far from where she was sleeping.

She enquired about it from the maid who had prepared her bath for her.

"We 'as a Service there sometimes, Miss," the maid said, "but t'Vicar likes us to go t'the Church in the Park."

"I would like to see the old Chapel," Lavela replied.

"It's easy enough, Miss," the maid told her. "If you slip down that staircase on t'other side o'the corridor there's a passage straight ahead o'you, an' the Chapel's at the end o'it."

"Thank you," Lavela said.

Now she thought that late though it was, she would like to pray in the Chapel.

It seemed appropriate that she should thank God there for all the Duke had done for her.

Her father had told her the Chapel had been built a hundred years before Moor Park was redesigned.

Opening her door she found the lights were still lit in the corridor and it was easy to find her way to the staircase.

There were also candles in silver sconces to show her the way down to the passage below.

She moved softly along the passage until she saw the Chapel door ahead of her.

There was a light shining through it.

She thought it strange that the Chapel should be lit at night.

At the same time, it was in keeping with the huge fires burning in every room.

As she reached the door of the Chapel she realised there was somebody inside.

Fearing she might be intruding, she stood still.

Then she heard a man's voice say harshly;

"You have to marry her, Sheldon, and there is nothing you can do about it!"

"I absolutely refuse!"

It was the Duke who spoke.

Surprised and at the same time frightened that something very strange was happening, Lavela moved a little nearer.

Now she could see that standing in front of the altar were three people.

One was the Duke, wearing a long robe like one her father wore over his nightshirt.

Then there was Lady Faversham looking, Lavela thought, exceedingly beautiful, and sparkling with jewels.

On the other side of the Duke was Joscelyn Moore, to whom she had been introduced earlier.

She had thought there was something unpleasant about him although he was good-looking.

When he had touched her hand she had known that he was evil.

Now she saw there was a revolver in his hand and he was pointing it at the Duke.

With an effort she prevented herself from screaming.

Then she saw that facing the three people was another man.

She had not noticed him at first because he was short and somehow insignificant.

He was wearing a surplice and she knew he was a Parson.

"You are in no position, Sheldon, to refuse to marry

Fiona," Joscelyn Moore was saying in the same harsh voice he had used before.

"You brought me down here by telling me there had been an accident to one of my staff," the Duke answered. "Now I intend to go back to bed, and if you have not left my house by breakfast-time tomorrow, I shall have you thrown out!"

Joscelyn Moore laughed, and it was a very unpleasant sound.

"Do you really believe, Sheldon, that you can defy me?" he asked. "I am pointing a fully loaded revolver at you."

"If you kill me you will hang," the Duke retorted, "and I cannot believe that is what you want."

"What I want," Joscelyn snarled, "is that you marry Fiona, whom you have most certainly compromised. That will ensure that I shall become the third Duke of Moorminster!"

"What makes you so sure of that?" the Duke enquired.

"Fiona tells me you know already that she cannot have a child," Joscelyn replied, "and although you are a young man, an accident might befall you which would save me from having to wait too long to attend your Funeral!"

"Do you really believe I am willing to go through the rest of my life expecting any moment that you will contrive somehow to cause my death?" the Duke said scornfully.

"I have already said you have no choice, and we are wasting time. If you do not marry Fiona, and the Clergyman is here ready to unite you two in Holy Matrimony, I will not hesitate to use this revolver!"

"And kill me?" the Duke asked mockingly.

Joscelyn shook his head.

"Oh, no!" he replied. "But I will maim you so that you

115

can never make love to a woman again, nor be capable of producing a child."

He almost spat the words at the Duke.

Lavela listening, shocked and horrified, wondered frantically what she could do to save the Duke.

Chapter Six

Lavela was hesitant.

She wondered if she should run to fetch somebody to rescue the Duke.

She was however, afraid that while she was gone he would be already married.

If only she could reach her father, she felt sure he would do something.

Even while she hesitated, Joscelyn Moore said to the Parson:

"Get on with it, and the quicker the better!"

The Parson opened his Prayer Book and Lavela knew there was no longer any time.

Hardly realising what she was doing she moved farther into the Chapel.

On either side of the door there was a pillar and standing on each an angel complete with wings.

The Duke had bought them in Bavaria.

They had been carved a hundred years earlier with that country's unique skill.

Then they had been painted in the soft colours which made every Bavarian Church a delight to the eye.

Lavela moved behind one of the pillars.

The Parson was beginning the Service.

"Dearly beloved . . "

"Cut out all that nonsense!" Joscelyn Moore ordered. "Get on to the Marriage Service itself."

"If the man knows what is best for him he will refuse to perform a Service which is illegal," the Duke warned, "and I shall not hesitate to take the matter to the Courts!"

Joscelyn laughed.

"And create a scandal? My dear Cousin, you know as well as I do that the one thing you have always been afraid of is anything that would shame our Noble Family!"

He spoke the last words mockingly and Fiona said:

"Be quiet, Joscelyn! There is no point in upsetting Sheldon more than he is already. All I want is to be his wife!"

"And that is what you will be," Joscelyn replied.

He looked again at the Parson.

"Do what you have been paid to do," he said, "otherwise I will have you defrocked, or whatever they do to punish creatures like you."

"I'm doing my best, Mr. Moore," the Parson said in a trembling voice.

He turned over two pages of his Prayer Book.

It was then that Lavela, who had been praying for help, knew what she must do.

She could feel the agony the Duke was going through in his mind.

She knew, almost as if he was telling her so, that he was trying to think of some way that he could knock his Cousin down and disarm him.

Anything to prevent this mockery of a marriage from taking place.

At the same time, the Duke was aware that Joscelyn was pointing his revolver straight at him below the waist.

His finger was on the trigger.

"Oh, my God, what can I do?" she asked silently.

"Help .. me! Please .. God .. help .. me!" Lavela prayed.

As she spoke she put up her hands and pushed at the angel in front of her.

For a moment she thought it was firmly attached to its stone pillar.

Then as she felt it move a little, she raised her hands higher and pushed with all the strength she could muster.

The angel moved, hovered, then toppled onto the stone floor with a loud crash.

It echoed round the Chapel walls.

Involuntarily Joscelyn turned to see what had happened.

It was the opportunity the Duke had been waiting for.

With his left hand he seized the revolver, thrusting it upwards.

At the same time, with the whole force of his very athletic body he struck Joscelyn a blow on the chin.

It was a punch that would have won the admiration of any Pugilist.

Joscelyn staggered, then fell backwards.

As he did so he pulled the trigger and a bullet shot upwards into the ceiling.

The explosion made even more noise than the falling angel.

It was added to by a shrill scream from Fiona.

Joscelyn's head had hit the stone floor as he fell, and he now lay still.

119

The Duke bent down and picked up the revolver.

It was lying a little way from his Cousin's body.

As he straightened himself the Parson cringed back against the altar saying in a quavering voice:

"He made me do it! He made me do it!"

The Duke gave him a contemptuous look and turned to Fiona.

As he did so the Night-watchman and the footman on duty in the hall came running into the Chapel.

They passed Lavela without seeing her.

She slid silently into the shadows at the side of the Chapel.

The Night-watchman reached the Duke first.

"Be ye all right, Yer Grace? Us 'eard a shot."

He looked as he spoke at the revolver in the Duke's hand.

"Nobody is injured," the Duke answered curtly.

Then as the footman came up beside the Night-watchman he asked:

"How did this Parson get here?"

" 'E come in a Post-Chaise, Yer Grace. It be waitin' fer 'im outside."

"Then take him to it," the Duke ordered, "and put Mr. Joscelyn in the carriage with him!"

The footman and the Night-watchman looked surprised.

Then obediently they walked to where Joscelyn was lying unconscious.

They picked him up, one taking his shoulders the other his legs.

The Duke watched them as they moved down the aisle.

With a gesture of his hand he indicated to the Parson to follow them.

120

He did so hurriedly passing the Duke as if he was afraid of being struck.

As he scuttled down the aisle the Duke said to Fiona:

"Because you are a woman, and it is late, I will not make you go with them. But you will leave this house first thing tomorrow morning!"

She moved towards him.

"How can you do this to me, Sheldon?" she pleaded. "I love you! I have always wanted to be your wife!"

"I am being merciful in not making you go with your lover," the Duke said sharply, "and I hope never to see you again!"

For a moment Fiona just stared at him.

Then as she realised what he said and that he knew about her and Joscelyn, her eyes flickered.

Defeated, she moved away holding her head high.

Only when she was out of sight did the Duke call softly;

"Lavela!"

He looked towards the dark corner where she had hidden herself.

Because she could not help it she ran towards him.

When she reached him she said breathlessly;

"I prayed . . I prayed . . desperately that I could . . help you!"

"You saved me," the Duke said quietly, "and I am more grateful than I can possibly say!"

He gave a deep sigh.

"I can hardly believe it all happened, and that you were there at exactly the right moment."

"I . . came down . . stairs to . . the Chapel because I . . wanted to say a . . prayer of gratitude for the . . wonderful evening," Lavela explained,

"but I think .. God must have sent me to ..
help you."

"I am quite sure of it," the Duke replied.

He put the revolver he still held in his hand down on
the nearest pew.

Then he said;

"I think we should offer our thanks together."

Lavela gave him a smile which made her look even
more like an angel.

Then as if she understood what he wanted she knelt
down on the altar steps.

The Duke joined her and they both closed their eyes.

Then as the Duke finished the most fervent prayer
he had ever said in his whole life, he put out his
hand.

He drew Lavela to her feet.

"You saved me!" he said again, as if he could hardly
believe himself it had actually happened.

"You do not .. think he will .. try to .. hurt
you again?" she whispered.

"I expect he will," the Duke replied, "and I can only
hope that when he does you, as my Guardian Angel,
will somehow manage to protect me."

"I will .. try .. you know I will .. try," Lavela
said, "but .. I am frightened."

She looked so lovely as she looked up at him with a
worried expression in her eyes that the Duke said;

"I have thanked God, but I think also, Lavela, I
should thank you!"

He put his arms round her as he spoke and bending
his head he kissed her.

It was a very gentle kiss, for he was not at the moment
thinking of her as an attractive woman.

122

She was an angel who had saved him from a fate that was too humiliating to contemplate.

Then as he felt the soft sweetness of Lavela's lips his kiss became more demanding, more possessive.

At the same time there was still a reverence about it.

To Lavela it was as if the Gates of Heaven had opened and she had been swept inside.

She had never been kissed, and she was astonished at the touch of the Duke's lips on hers.

She thought it was very wonderful that somebody so magnificent and marvellous as the Duke should actually kiss her.

Then she felt a strange sensation she had never known before.

It was as if the light from the stars was twinkling inside her.

She knew that the same light enveloped both the Duke and herself, and it was the light of God.

Without being conscious of doing so, she moved her body closer to his.

His arms tightened and the sensations within her increased.

They were so intense, so perfect, and at the same time so Divine that she knew this was Love.

This was a love unbelievable, amazing and overwhelming.

As the Duke's lips became more possessive she felt she was no longer herself, but his.

When he raised his head to look down at her the Duke thought he had never seen anyone look so radiant.

At the same time so beautiful.

As she looked up at him he knew she was not

thinking of him as a man, but as someone she worshipped.

"My Darling, how can you make me feel like this?"
he asked.

Then he was kissing her again.

Kissing her now as if she was no longer an angel, but
a woman who was utterly and completely desirable.

Because they were in the Chapel and had passed
through a gruelling experience, he knew that what he
felt for Lavela was very different from what he had felt
for any other woman.

He kissed her again, but now more gently.

Then he said:

"I think it would be a great mistake for anyone, to
know what has happened here tonight."

"Will not .. the servants .. talk?" Lavela asked
hesitatingly.

"I will make sure they do not!" the Duke answered.

He looked at her very tenderly. Then he said:

"I want you to go to bed and forget this happened
to spoil your happy evening, which you enjoyed so
much."

"How can I forget it .. when you .. are still ..
in danger?" Lavela murmured.

"For the moment I am quite safe," the Duke answered,
"and my disreputable Cousin will not be in a position to
hurt anyone for at least 48 hours!"

"B .. but .. after that .. ?"

"After that I shall rely on you, and of course God, to
keep me safe," the Duke said simply.

He spoke with a sincerity which would have surprised
him at any other time.

It brought the light back into Lavela's eyes.

124

"I will do what you say," she said, "but . . promise you will be . . careful."

"We will talk about that tomorrow," the Duke answered.

He took her by the hand and they walked out of the Chapel, leaving the candles burning.

At the bottom of the stairs which led up to the floor on which Lavela was sleeping the Duke kissed her again and said;

"Goodnight, my Darling, dream happy dreams and forget the nightmare we have just passed through."

"I will . . dream of . . you," Lavela answered.

Then because she knew he was waiting, she walked up the stairs.

He watched her from below until she reached the top.

She waved to him and when she had disappeared from his sight he walked to the hall.

As he expected, the Night-watchman and the footman were waiting.

The front door was still open, letting in the cold night air.

The Duke could see a Post-Chaise drawn by two horses in the distance.

It went over the bridge which spanned the lake.

It vanished from sight under the branches of the ancient oak trees which lined either side of the long drive.

When he could see it no longer he said sharply;

"Shut the door!"

The footman obeyed him and thrust home two bolts besides turning the key in the lock.

The Duke then spoke more quietly.

He told them what had happened tonight was not to be repeated to anyone in the house or outside.

He said that if they disobeyed him they would be instantly dismissed without a reference.

"That is something I have never said before to anyone in my employment," he said, "but as this is a very serious matter, I want you to promise me on your word of honour that you will never speak of it to anyone."

"Oi gives yer me word o' honour, Yer Grace!" the Night-watchman said, and the footman echoed him.

Then when the Duke would have walked away he asked:

"Where did that Post-Chaise come from?"

"From London, Yer Grace, an' th' driver tells Oi it took nigh on four hours in comin' 'ere 'cause th' Reverend Gent kep' stoppin' at every Inn on the way to 'ave a drink!"

The Duke did not say anything, and the footman added:

"The driver, Your Grace, asks fer a mug o' ale when 'e gets 'ere an' Oi give 'im one, an' before he goes orf 'e were singin'!"

The Duke thought such behaviour was what he might have expected of the type of Clergyman that Joscelyn would employ.

He knew it was always possible to find one in London who would marry couples late at night.

They were in regular demand by unscrupulous women who had trapped some rich drunkard into matrimony when he had no idea of what he was doing.

Had he been married to Fiona he might not have been able to prove the ceremony was illegal.

At the same time, as Joscelyn was aware, he would have found it hard to face the distress an attempt to do so would cause to his family.

As he walked upstairs to his bedroom he wondered how he could ever be grateful enough for having escaped.

It was a baited trap which would undoubtedly have ruined his whole life.

As he got into bed he was thinking of Lavela.

Not only of how beautiful she was, but also how clever.

No other woman could have thought of a way of preventing the marriage.

Joscelyn had planned it so craftily.

When his cousin had come into his bedroom he had said in an agitated voice;

"There has been an accident, Sheldon, in the Chapel, of all unlikely places, and I think you had better come quickly!"

Mention of the Chapel immediately brought Lavela to the Duke's mind and he asked;

"Who is it? What has happened?"

"There is no time to talk," Joscelyn replied, "just follow me as fast as you can."

He had gone ahead and the Duke had been unable to ask any more questions.

When he reached the Chapel he had found Fiona there.

Then Joscelyn produced a revolver and he realised that he had been caught.

He thought now it was somehow appropriate that Lavela, who looked so like an angel, had used one to save him.

He was very proud of his two Bavarian angels.

He only hoped the one which now lay on the stone floor could be skilfully repaired.

But nothing really mattered except that he was safe, at least for the moment.

And that he loved Lavela.

"I am too old for her to be interested in me!" he told himself.

Then he knew from the way she had responded to his kiss, the way she had moved closer in his arms, that she loved him.

It was as he had wanted to be loved.

Not merely because he was a Duke.

From the moment they had prayed together there had been a close affinity between them, but he had not realised at first it was love.

It was a very different love from what he had ever felt before.

That was why he had not recognised it.

It was not the wild burning fire of passion.

That was something completely physical and what he had felt for Fiona and the women before her.

He knew now that Lavela worshipped him as he worshipped her.

She was everything that was perfect in a woman.

He knew without her telling him that she loved him not only with her heart, but also with her soul.

The Duke had not thought of his soul until now; but if he possessed one, he knew it was hers.

Before he fell asleep he was thinking that no one could be more blessed than he was.

At the same time, he was wondering what his family would say.

They would obviously disapprove when he told them

he was going to marry the daughter of the Vicar of Little Bedlington.

The Duke woke early.

His first thought was that he must make sure that Fiona obeyed his instructions.

He hoped she would leave the house before she could come in contact with any of his other guests.

As she had been humiliated he thought it unlikely that she would want to talk.

Yet one could never trust a woman not to be indiscreet.

He therefore rang for his Valet, and when he came sent him to fetch Mr. Watson.

He instructed Mr. Watson that Lady Faversham was to leave on the first available train which could be stopped at the Halt.

The Housekeeper was to see that all her things were packed.

After that the Duke thought he need never again concern himself with Fiona.

Instead he could think of Lavela.

Now in the light of day the difficulties of marrying her seemed to close in on him like vultures.

He was worried not for himself but for her.

He knew only too well that his family would be upset.

They would be horrified that he was not marrying somebody whose blood was the equal of his own.

Someone who would fill the position of Duchess with dignity.

That could hardly be expected from a girl who had seldom been out of the village of Little Bedlington.

They might even be unkind and rude to her.

The Duke knew how women, especially older women, could intimidate and humiliate a young girl.

Especially one for whom they had no respect.

Every instinct in his body made him want to protect Lavela.

Not so much from physical injury as from anything that would hurt her spiritually and mentally.

He hated the thought that her trust in other people might be destroyed.

She had always lived in a house of love.

She had never come up against the envy, hatred and malice of the Social World.

Nor the cruelty a woman could inflict on another woman.

It was not only by what might be said, but the way that they thought about her.

The Duke knew the first thing he must do was to prevent anybody knowing what he and Lavela felt for each other.

It must be an absolute secret until the house-party and the Opening of the Theatre were over.

He wanted the audience to look at Lavela as a beautiful singing angel.

Not as a local girl who had managed by some skilful means of her own, to capture a Duke.

He therefore sent his Valet with a note to tell the maid who was looking after Lavela that he wished to see her in the Theatre immediately.

He knew his request would be taken at its face value and that it concerned Lavela's performance.

He waited for her in one of the boxes.

Five minutes later she came speeding through the door which led from the house.

130

For a moment she did not see him.

He watched her as she looked round the Theatre.

She had an expression of expectation in her eyes which made his heart turn a somersault.

Then as he spoke her name very softly she saw him in the box beside her.

She gave a little cry of delight.

Spontaneously, without thinking, she flung herself into his arms.

As he held her against him she asked:

"Is it true . . really true . . what you . . said last night . . that you . . love me?"

"I adore you!" the Duke confirmed in a deep voice.

She smiled.

"When I first . . woke up I thought it . . could not be . . true and that I had . . only been dreaming."

"That is what I felt too," he said.

Then he kissed her until they were both breathless.

"Now listen, my precious," he said at last, "I think it would be a great mistake, and I know you will think the same, that anyone should know how much we love each other until after tomorrow evening."

"Yes . . of course . . I understand," Lavela said "I want people to think about your . . music Play and realise how . . clever you are."

"That is what we hope they will think!" the Duke smiled. "And when my family has left and everybody else with them, then we can think about ourselves."

She smiled at him.

She was even lovelier than he had thought her to be yesterday.

"I love you!" he said. "All I want is to keep telling you so, but we both know we have a lot of work to do."

131

Lavela nodded.

Then in a different tone of voice she asked:

"You have . . made sure that . . no one will talk about . . what happened . . last night?"

"Absolutely sure," the Duke affirmed, "so do not think about it today. You just have to concentrate on rehearsing the children."

"Yes, of course," she agreed.

The Duke kissed her again.

Then he said:

"Now we will both be very, very careful that no one guesses our precious secret. But if you look at me as you are doing now, we shall be unable to hide it!"

"Then I will . . try not to look at you," Lavela answered seriously, "but it will be difficult because I keep thinking you are . . too wonderful to be . . real."

"I am very real, and I love you, just as you love me," the Duke said. "But now we must get back to reality, and that is – breakfast!"

Lavela laughed.

"I feel we should be eating nothing but Ambrosia which is far more romantic than eggs and bacon!"

The Duke kissed her again.

Then he took her from the Theatre back into the house.

As Lavela made her way to the Breakfast-Room he went to his Study.

Mr. Watson was there waiting to see him which he thought was unusual as he did not normally send for him so early.

"I am afraid I bring you bad news," Mr. Watson said.

132

"What is it?" the Duke enquired.

"I have just been informed, Your Grace, that there was an accident last night at the cross-roads outside the village."

The Duke was still.

"What happened?" he enquired.

"A Post-Chaise containing Mr. Joscelyn and a Clergyman came into collision with the Carrier's cart!"

The Duke waited.

"According to the Carrier, Your Grace, the driver of the Post-Chaise was drunk and whipping up his horses in the most reckless manner."

"Go on," the Duke prompted.

"The Post-Chaise was overturned," Mr. Watson continued. "The Clergyman had a broken leg, but I regret to tell Your Grace that Mr. Joscelyn was very badly injured and is in a coma."

"He is alive?" the Duke questioned thinking his voice sounded strange as he did so.

"The Doctor says there is no chance of saving him, but he and the Clergyman have been taken to a Hospital."

The Duke sat down at his desk.

He could not be so hypocritical as to pretend that if Joscelyn died it would be anything but a relief.

At the same time, it was something of a shock to realise that in sending him away as he had done, he was partly responsible.

"I was wondering," Mr. Watson said, "if as their Royal Highnesses are arriving today, it would be best for nothing to be said about Mr. Joscelyn's condition until after the Performance tomorrow evening?"

"Yes, of course – you are right," the Duke agreed.

"Doctor Graham is awaiting Your Grace's instructions. He recognised Mr. Joscelyn, but as he was in evening clothes no one else knew he was staying, and the Doctor did not enlighten them."

The Duke knew Dr. Graham.

He was an elderly man who had attended his father and himself and any members of his family who needed his services when they stayed at Moor Park.

He realised the Doctor was being very tactful and understanding.

He knew it would ruin the Christmas house-party and be uncomfortable when they were entertaining the Prince and Princess of Wales anticipating Joscelyn's death.

Dr. Graham being so closely associated with the Moores, was doubtless aware of Joscelyn's disreputable behaviour.

Of course the village was talking about the way he threw money away on riotous living.

"I will call on Dr. Graham myself as soon as I have had breakfast," the Duke said aloud.

"That is what I thought Your Grace would say," Mr. Watson replied.

"He is right, of course," the Duke went on. "It would be extremely awkward and would certainly spoil the party and our Show tomorrow night if anyone knew what has happened."

Dr. Graham said that only a few of the villagers knew there had been an accident, and they had no idea the Post-Chaise had anything to do with him.

"I am extremely grateful for Dr. Graham's discretion," the Duke said, "and thank goodness, Watson, I can rely on yours."

Mr. Watson smiled and the Duke left the Study to go to the Breakfast-Room.

As he did so he was thinking that Lavela would not need to tell him again that he had to be grateful.

He was very, very grateful that Fate or God, had been so generous to him.

Chapter Seven

Their Royal Highnesses arrived on Friday evening.

They were extremely courteous to all the members of the Duke's family.

The Duke, however, was watching Lavela's reaction.

He thought the excitement in her eyes was like that of a child at a Pantomime.

Almost immediately the party went up to dress for dinner.

The Chef, as excited as everybody else, excelled himself. Each course was a poem in itself.

It was not the first time the Prince had stayed at Moor Park.

It was however, the first time he had done so with the Princess.

"I am so looking forward to the opening of your Theatre," Princess Alexandra said in her sweet voice to the Duke, "and I am sure you have something delightful in store for us."

"I only hope you will like it, Ma'am," the Duke said. "It is certainly unusual."

As he spoke he remembered that the Princess was very musical.

Being very poor before her father came to the throne of Denmark, she had been taught by her mother.

The Queen was a member of the Hesse-Cassel family, and all her six children were extremely talented.

The Duke was sure that Princess Alexandra would be impressed that at the Opening of the Theatre all the performers came from one small village.

When the gentlemen joined the ladies after dinner the Duke heaved a sigh of relief that Fiona was no longer there.

There was no need for him now to be afraid that she would enlist the Prince's help in forcing him to marry her.

Nor need he be worried that Joscelyn would do anything to offend the rest of the family.

As he came into the Drawing-Room he saw, to his surprise, that Lavela was sitting beside Princess Alexandra.

They were talking animatedly.

He could not help thinking it extraordinary that someone as young and unsophisticated as Lavela should not seem nervous or in any way shy at being in the presence of Royalty.

In fact as he watched her she appeared to be completely at ease.

Both she and the Princess were laughing when he walked across the room to join them.

"I am curious, Your Royal Highness," he said, "as to what Lavela is saying to make you laugh."

"We were actually talking about Musicians and their strange idiosyncracies when they are performing," the Princess replied.

The Duke raised his eyebrows and Lavela explained:

"I was telling Her Royal Highness about one of Papa's friends who was a most distinguished violinist. He had a strange habit of kissing the handkerchief he put under his chin on which to rest his instrument, because he thought it would bring him luck!"

"And I was telling Miss Ashley," the Princess chimed in, "about one of our most distinguished pianists in Denmark who carries a spider in a box in his pocket, which he always uses when he is gambling."

The Duke laughed and said:

"Now I think about it, a great number of famous people have strange ideas like that. Perhaps we should collect them and publish them in a book."

The Princess laughed, but Lavela said;

"If they read it, it would only make them nervous, and then perhaps they would not be able to play as well in the future."

The Duke thought it was a nice thing to say and he smiled at her.

Then as she smiled back he remembered that they were supposed to appear indifferent towards each other.

Everybody went to bed early.

The Duke was sure a great number of his guests were lying awake thinking of what they would do tomorrow.

He wanted to be with Lavela and help her to rehearse the children who were sleeping in the East Wing.

He had arranged that the Princess should have a guided tour of the house.

Also that the Prince should visit the stables and be shown the horses.

Because both of the Royal Couple had been very busy the previous week and over Christmas he guessed they would not wish to exert themselves unnecessarily.

He had in fact asked if the Prince would like a Shoot.

The reply was that His Royal Highness had a sore arm after a very arduous day's shooting at Sandringham.

The Prince would therefore rather have a quiet day.

This suited the Duke, who had no wish to shoot when he had so much to do in the Theatre.

He knew he must be present as host if His Royal Highness was one of the guns.

The next morning he left his relations to look after themselves.

He found Lavela in the Theatre conducting the children from the Orchestra Pit while they sang their Carol on the stage.

She had improvised something since he had last been present.

In between the verses they joined hands and danced around in a circle.

Because the children were so small it looked very attractive.

It was too in keeping with the stage itself where the Duke had arranged flowers at the back and on each side.

Big pots of lilies concealed much of the grand pianos.

He had always thought they were not particularly attractive instruments.

They had been pushed to each side so that the audience would only just see the two pianists.

The Duke also arranged that when they had finished the Overture the pianos could be pulled back still further by unseen hands off-stage.

He walked down the centre aisle to stand behind Lavela.

She was very conscious of him.

Finally the last verse of the Carol came to an end and the children walked forward to curtsy gracefully.

The Duke clapped his hands.

"Bravo!" he said. "I know tonight you will receive tremendous applause. In that case, you must curtsy for a second time before the curtains are pulled to."

The children understood, and as they went from the stage he put his hand on Lavela's shoulder.

"I love you!" he said very softly.

She looked up at him.

There was no need for her to speak or tell him what she felt about him.

"You are not nervous?" he asked.

"Only in case .. you are .. disappointed," she answered.

That, he was certain, would not happen.

The Duke had arranged because the children were so young that the performance would take place before dinner.

At six o'clock the audience were taking their places in the Theatre.

The Prince and Princess entered when everybody else was seated and they all stood for *God Save The Queen*.

The lights were then extinguished in the auditorium and the Duke and Lavela began the Overture.

The applause they received at the end of it was very gratifying.

Then the Vicar, well disguised as Harlequin recited his welcoming and very amusing poem.

The curtains drew back to show the children grouped to resemble a bouquet of flowers, which caused a murmur of delight.

After that the Programme was as professional as

anything that might have been seen on the London stage.

The Duke's episode was outstanding, and he felt it was a pity there was to be only the one performance of it.

He knew that Maria Colzaio was singing as brilliantly as she had done in all the great Opera Houses in Europe.

She did not however, outshine Lavela.

She looked so lovely as the Angel that it was difficult for him to think of anybody else.

The words of her song were very moving:

"One thing I know, life can never die,
    Translucent, splendid, flaming like the sun.
Only our bodies wither and deny
    The life force when our strength is done."

The song went on to tell the listeners that her good deeds and the love she had given while she was on earth would live for ever.

When finally the curtain closed on the play there was that appreciative silence for which every artist longs.

It is the greatest accolade they can receive.

Then the applause rang out and the Prince of Wales was heard to cry;

"Bravo! Bravo!"

As the Duke thought, after that everything went on well-oiled wheels.

Finally he appeared as Father Christmas.

The children ran down from the stage to distribute the presents, which was a surprise to everyone.

He had given Mr. Watson *carte blanche* to buy what presents he thought suitable.

Nobody was disappointed with what they received.

The Male Voice Choir singing behind him sang *God Rest Ye Merry Gentlemen*.

141

Then finally the children went back onto the stage and the curtain fell, there was another burst of applause.

Then the Prince and Princess told the Duke they would like to meet the Performers.

The red curtains were therefore drawn back again and Their Royal Highnesses walked down from the box and onto the stage.

They congratulated everyone in their usual charming manner.

The Duke took off his Father Christmas robes and escorted them from the stage and up the aisle which led to the house.

They had almost reached the steps which would take them there when Princess Alexandra stopped suddenly.

Sitting with the five mothers of the performing children in the last row of the Stalls was Mrs. Ashley.

The Princess was staring at her.

The Duke wondered if he should introduce her when the Princess exclaimed:

"Louise! It *is* Louise?"

Mrs. Ashley with a little sob held out her arms.

To the Duke's amazement the next minute the two women were kissing each other, and there were tears in their eyes.

"Louise! I have found you! I have found you! I have missed you so terribly all these years!"

"As I missed you, Alex," Mrs. Ashley said.

The Prince and the Duke were looking in astonishment at what was occurring.

The rest of the audience had turned round to stare too.

As if she was suddenly aware of it, Princess Alexandra said to the Prince:

"Darling, this is my Cousin Louise Hesse-Cassel, who

142

ran away years ago and we had no idea where she had gone!"

"I can imagine your surprise at finding her here!" the Prince said. "You must tell us the whole story."

The Duke took charge.

"I think we would be more comfortable, if we went into the house," he said, "and, as Your Highness is aware, dinner is waiting."

"Louise must come with us," Princess Alexandra said quickly.

"Of course," the Duke replied, "and Your Royal Highness has already met Mrs. Ashley's charming husband and her beautiful daughter Lavela."

The Princess took Mrs. Ashley by the hand.

"How could you have gone away like that, Louise? I cried and cried for nights after you left?"

"Oh, dearest Alex, I did not want to hurt you," Mrs. Ashley answered, "but I was so very much in love!"

The Princess laughed.

"Then that means, of course, that I shall have to forgive you!"

They went up the steps together followed by the Prince and the Duke who could hardly believe what he had just heard.

If Mrs. Ashley was, as the Princess had said, her Cousin, it would make it easy for him to marry Lavela with the full approval of the Moore family.

The Duke could not tell Lavela what he had planned until after the Royal Couple had left Moor Park on Sunday.

143

It had been snowing all the previous evening but now the sun had come out.

It made the park and gardens and the great house look even more beautiful than they did usually.

Mrs. Ashley spent the night with them but not only because the Princess wished her to do so.

It was snowing hard by the time dinner came to an end.

The Duke was informed that his coachman considered it too dangerous to take the horses out and almost impossible to reach Little Bedlington.

Maria Colzaio was therefore another guest.

As she was fêted and congratulated by everyone in the house-party the Duke was sure she would, in the future, no longer wish to remain incognito.

What interested him most was that he had found the answer to what had been puzzling him about the Ashleys.

For the first time he learned that Andrew Ashley was the younger son of Lord Ashbrook.

He had been ordained after leaving Oxford.

He had insisted however, before he accepted one of the Livings on his father's estate, that he would explore the world first.

He had therefore left England for nearly three years.

He had travelled all over Europe, visited the East and on his way home, went to St. Petersburg.

From there he journeyed to Denmark.

"The moment I saw Louise," the Vicar said, "I knew she was the one person I had been looking for all my life."

"And I felt the same about Andrew," Mrs. Ashley said softly.

"It was very cruel of you to steal her away from us!" Princess Alexandra said accusingly.

"It was impossible, Ma'am, for me to leave her behind," the Vicar replied.

Mrs. Ashley put up her hand.

"You must not be unkind to Andrew. He tried to save me from himself, but we both knew how utterly miserable we would be for the rest of our lives."

"You have been happy?" Princess Alexandra asked.

"So blissfully, over-whelmingly happy," Mrs. Ashley answered, "that I never for one moment regretted running away, except, dearest Alex, that I missed you."

The Duke listening could hardly believe that this was all happening.

He realised however, that what he felt for Lavela was exactly the same as her father and mother had felt for each other.

They had run away and he knew it was something he too had to do.

When Joscelyn died it would be impossible for there to be a wedding in the family for at least six months.

Queen Victoria would expect it to be longer.

He moved from the Blue Drawing-Room where the Royal Couple and the Ashleys were talking intimately and went to find Mr. Watson.

Having given him a list of instructions he went into the Salon where all his family were gathered.

They were all immensely curious to discover what was happening.

When he told them who the Vicar they admired so much actually was, they said they were not in the least surprised.

"He is such a good-looking man and so charming!" one of the Duke's Aunts said. "I felt he could not just be an ordinary Vicar of Little Bedlington."

The Duke knew that was exactly what they would have said if he had married Lavela without her Royal connections.

"It has been one of the best parties you have ever given!" the Prince of Wales declared when he said goodbye.

"It has been a great honour to have you here, Sir!" the Duke responded.

Princess Alexandra was kissing Mrs. Ashley.

"You must promise me, Louise," she said, "that you will come and see us at Marlborough House. And the next time we go to Sandringham all three of you must be our guests."

"Of course we will come, dearest Alex," Mrs. Ashley said, "and you know I want to see your children."

"We will give a special Ball for Lavela later in the Season," the Princess promised.

When the Royal Couple had departed the Duke took Lavela's hand in his and said to the Vicar and Mrs. Ashley:

"I would like you to come to my Study, as there is something important I want to tell you."

The Vicar and his wife were surprised.

But they followed the Duke, who still kept Lavela's hand in his, down the passage to the Study.

Newton opened the door and as the Duke entered he said:

"Stay outside the door, Newton. I do not wish to be disturbed."

"Very good, Your Grace."

The door shut and the Duke walked to the fireplace and stood with his back to the fire.

The Ashleys sat down, but Lavela stayed beside him.

He released her hand and she sat down on a chair looking up at him, he thought a little apprehensively.

"Lavela and I," the Duke announced, "wish to be married immediately!"

"Married?" Mrs. Ashley exclaimed looking at her daughter. "Oh, Darling, why did you not tell me?"

Lavela jumped up kneeling beside her mother's chair, and Mrs. Ashley kissed her.

"It is everything I could wish for you," she said, "as long as it will make you happy."

"It is the most . . wonderful thing that could ever . . happen," Lavela murmured.

The Vicar rose, put out his hand and said:

"There is no man to whom I would rather entrust my daughter than yourself!"

"Thank you," the Duke replied. "At the same time, there is some difficulty about it, and I need your help."

He then told them very briefly what had happened last night.

He also was truthful about the part Fiona had played in his life.

At the same time he made it clear that, while she had wanted to marry him, he had had no intention of marrying anyone until he met Lavela.

"That is exactly what I felt about Louise," the Vicar murmured.

"Then you will understand that I was only waiting to tell her how much she meant to me until this evening was over."

The Vicar nodded.

"However, this morning," the Duke went on, "I learnt something which could prevent us from being married for a long time."

Lavela, who was still kneeling beside her mother's chair, gave a little cry.

"But . . why? What has . . happened?"

"Last night after Joscelyn left here," the Duke explained, "he and that disreputable Parson of his were involved in an accident."

"An accident?" the Vicar exclaimed.

The Duke repeated what Mr. Watson had told him.

The Parson had a broken leg, but there was no hope of saving Joscelyn's life and he would die within a few days.

The three people listening were silent and the Duke went on quietly;

"You will understand that if he dies I shall be in mourning for my Cousin."

He paused a moment and then went on:

"It will be impossible for me to marry in the near future without arousing a great deal of criticism and certainly the disapproval of the Moore family."

"Yes, of course, I understand that," Mrs. Ashley said. "So you and Lavela will have to wait."

"On the contrary," the Duke said, "like you and your husband, we are going to run away!"

He smiled before he added:

"You set a precedent, so you can hardly blame us if we do the same!"

"What are . . we going . . to do?" Lavela asked.

"Your father is going to marry us first thing tomorrow morning," the Duke said, "and we shall leave here immediately."

Lavela's face was radiant as she rose to her feet.

"Can we . . do that? Can we really do . . that?" she gasped.

148

The Duke put his arms around her when she was standing beside him.

"It is what we are going to do," he said, "and we are going on a very long honeymoon. There are so many places in the world I want to show you, and so many things we can do together."

She was smiling up at him as he looked down at her.

They were both obviously so happy that tears came into Mrs. Ashley's eyes.

She put out her hand towards her husband.

"You are quite right," the Vicar said quietly.

"It is what I intended to do anyway," the Duke went on. "A long engagement would only allow my relatives to frighten Lavela by telling her what a bad husband I will be!"

He spoke teasingly, but Lavela replied seriously:

"You do not imagine I would . . listen to . . them?"

"Now you are going to find out for yourself whether I am good or bad!" the Duke smiled.

Lavela gave a little cry of happiness and put her cheek against his arm.

"I will see that everything is ready for you," the Vicar said, "and as you do not wish anyone to know about the ceremony I suggest we meet at your Chapel at eight o'clock."

"That is what I thought myself," the Duke replied. "Some of my relations are leaving this afternoon and the rest intend to depart tomorrow morning."

"It must be . . kept a secret . . until we have . . actually left . . the house," Lavela said.

"Of course," the Duke agreed, "and I know your father and mother understand that. Luckily my relatives have quite enough to talk about already!"

149

He smiled at Mrs. Ashley as he spoke and said:

"I felt there was some mystery about you and your husband, and wondered why you buried yourselves in Little Bedlington. I was curious – but I never expected to find the answer in such a dramatic fashion!"

"I thought Alex would not recognise me after so many years," Mrs. Ashley answered.

"If anyone had once seen you it would be impossible for them ever to forget you, my Darling!" the Vicar said.

His wife slipped her hand into his.

"I think, Dearest, you are prejudiced," she smiled. "At the same time, I am very happy to have found Alex again, and she says she is sure her father and mother will forgive me. Then we will be able to go and stay in Denmark and of course with my family in Germany."

"And what is going to happen to Little Bedlington," the Duke asked, "if you are going to be travelling abroad and becoming a part of London Society?"

The Vicar laughed and replied:

"That is quite easy. You and Lavela will have to keep up the high musical standards we have set in the village, and perhaps you could extend it over your whole Estate."

"That is a challenge," Lavela said before the Duke could speak.

"I will certainly think about it," the Duke replied, "but quite frankly at the moment all I want is to have Lavela to myself."

. . . . . .

The Duke and Duchess of Moorminster drove away from Moor Park at eight-thirty the following morning.

There was no one to see them off except the servants, the Vicar and Mrs. Ashley.

"God bless you, my Darling," the Vicar said as he kissed Lavela goodbye.

"He has done that already by giving me such a wonderful husband," Lavela replied.

She looked very lovely as she seated herself beside the Duke in his Travelling-Carriage.

It was drawn by four perfectly matched horses.

There were two out-riders to accompany them.

The pale sun was just rising in the sky.

It made Lavela, the Duke thought, look like an angel who had come down from Heaven to be with him.

He knew while they were being married that he was starting a new chapter in his life.

It would be very different in every way from anything he had done before.

The Chapel on his instructions had been transformed from what it had been the night when Joscelyn had tried to force him to marry Fiona.

It had now looked like a bower of love.

There were lilies on the altar and flowers of every colour and description arranged round the walls.

There was no one else present except Mrs. Ashley.

But the Duke knew that for Lavela the angels were singing overhead, and he thought he himself recognised the tune.

When they knelt for the Blessing he was saying in his heart words of gratitude which he knew Lavela was also saying in hers.

"How can we have been so fortunate as to have found each other?" he asked. "And for the future to be as golden as the sunlight?"

Fortunately the snow had stopped falling before dawn and there was no frost.

The roads therefore were not dangerous.

As they sped through a white world the Duke thought it looked as pure as Lavela herself.

"I love you, my Darling!" he said.

"As I love you."

She spoke in the same rapt little voice with which she had made her responses in the Marriage Service.

Very gently the Duke took off the small hat she was wearing and put it down on the seat beside them.

Then he pulled her close against him and said:

"We have run away – we have escaped! Now nobody can prevent us from being together and I no longer have to be careful how I look at you."

Lavela laughed.

"I was so afraid that people would see me looking at you and know I was longing to be close as we are now."

"We are not yet close enough," the Duke said.

He saw his wife blush and added:

"Tonight we are staying in a house on the Dover Road which is my own but which I have only used when I have been going abroad."

"Do you realise," Lavela asked, "that I have not asked you where we are going? There has never been time."

"I have planned everything," the Duke said, "but I want it to be a surprise. You just have to shut your eyes until I tell you to open them."

She laughed.

"I am quite happy to do that as long as when I do . . open my eyes . . you will be . . there."

"You can be quite certain of that," the Duke answered.

The house which they reached late in the afternoon was small, but very comfortable.

The Duke had bought it from a friend because he disliked staying at Hotels.

It was too far for his horses to reach Dover in one day.

He liked to think he could slip across the Channel whenever he grew bored.

But what usually happened was that he went on a special Mission to Europe for either the Queen or the Prime Minister.

It was then he found his house convenient.

It pleased him to think he had never taken any other woman there.

Lavela was enchanted.

"It is like a doll's-house!" she exclaimed.

"I wanted you to think it was a Palace and I was 'Prince Charming'!" the Duke teased.

"You know you are that," she said, "and always will be, whether we are at Moor Park or in a cave! You will be you, and that is . . all that . . matters!"

It was what the Duke had always wanted and thought he would never find.

A woman who loved him for himself and not because of his title or possessions.

When later in the evening the Duke had undressed and went into Lavela's room he thought she would be in bed.

Instead she was standing at the window.

The curtains were drawn back so that she could look out.

The snow was quite thick on the ground, but the stars had come out in the sky.

A nearly full moon was rising over the trees.

Its light gave the world beneath it a magical ether-eal look.

It was difficult to believe it was the Earth and not some spiritual Paradise in which they were the only living creatures.

The Duke walked across the room and put his arms round Lavela.

"When you look away from me like that," he said, "I am half-afraid you will vanish back to where you came from and I shall never be able to find you again."

"You will never lose me now," Lavela said. "I knew when we were being married that we became not two people, but one, and now I am . . a part of you as . . you are a part of . . me."

The Duke kissed her forehead and lifting her up in his arms he carried her to the big silk-canopied bed.

He put her down against the pillows.

She looked across the room to where through the window she could still see the stars.

The Duke joined her and as he took her in his arms she asked:

"Is . . it true . . really true that we . . are here . . together . . and the moon and the . . stars are giving . . us their . . blessing?"

"It is really true," the Duke said, "and I will love you, my Darling, until the stars fall from the sky and the seas run dry!"

Then he was kissing her; kissing her very gently, so as not to frighten her.

Then as he felt her lips respond to his and her body quiver against him, his kisses became more passionate, possessive and demanding.

154

It was then he knew that the blood was pulsating in his temples.

A fire arose within him because he wanted Lavela to be his.

Yet at the same time his love was different from anything he had ever known before.

He knew, because Lavela was so young and innocent, that he must be very gentle with her and not hurt or frighten her.

He knew too because their love was so perfect that everything he did would be a part of the Divine.

"I love you! Oh God, how I love you!" he exclaimed.

"I feel . . when . . you are . . kissing me," Lavela whispered, "as if the . . stars are . . shining in my . . heart."

"That is what I want them to do."

Then as the Duke kissed her again he felt that he had awoken a response within her.

It was turning the shining stars into little flames of fire.

There was a great deal he had to teach her.

It would make them even happier than they were at this moment.

This he thought was like their Overture in the Theatre.

It heralded a wonder and beauty of something which came from Heaven itself.

"I love you . . oh . . Sheldon . . I love you!" Lavela was saying. "When you . . kiss me . . I feel as if I am . . flying in the . . sky!"

Something broke within the Duke and his kisses became more passionate.

He kissed her eyes, her lips, the softness of her neck and the little valley between her breasts.

Then, as he made Lavela his, he knew that together they touched the stars.

The light from them enveloped them both.

They were no longer human but with God in a Heaven which would be theirs for all Eternity.

Other books by Barbara Cartland

Romantic Novels, over 400, the most recently published being:

Love is the Key	The Scent of Roses
Free as the Wind	Love at First Sight
Desire in the Desert	The Secret Princess
A Heart in the Highlands	Heaven in Hong Kong
The Music of Love	Paradise in Penang
The Wrong Duchess	A Game of Love
The Taming of a Tigress	The Sleeping Princess
Love Comes to the Castle	A Wish Comes True
The Magic of Paris	Loved for Himself
Stand and Deliver your Heart	Two Hearts in Hungary

The Dream and the Glory (In aid of the St. John Ambulance Brigade)

Autobiographical and Biographical:

The Isthmus Years 1919–1939
The Years of Opportunity 1939–1945
I Search for Rainbows 1945–1976
We Danced All Night 1919–1929
Ronald Cartland (With a foreword by Sir Winston Churchill)
Polly – My Wonderful Mother
I Seek the Miraculous

Historical:

Bewitching Women
The Outrageous Queen (The Story of Queen Christina of Sweden)
The Scandalous Life of King Carol
The Private Life of Charles II
The Private Life of Elizabeth, Empress of Austria
Josephine, Empress of France
Diane de Poitiers
Metternich – The Passionate Diplomat
Royal Jewels
Royal Lovers
Royal Eccentrics
A Year of Royal Days

Sociology:

You in the Home	Etiquette
The Fascinating Forties	The Many Facets of Love
Marriage for Moderns	Sex and the Teenager
Be Vivid, Be Vital	The Book of Charm
Love, Life and Sex	Living Together
Vitamins for Vitality	The Youth Secret
Husbands and Wives	The Magic of Honey
Men are Wonderful	The Book of Beauty and Health

Keep Young and Beautiful by Barbara Cartland and Elinor Glyn
Etiquette for Love and Romance
Barbara Cartland's Book of Health

General:

Barbara Cartland's Book of Useless Information with a Foreword by the
   Earl Mountbatten of Burma.
   (In aid of the United World Colleges)
Love and Lovers (Picture Book)
The Light of Love (Prayer Book)
Barbara Cartland's Scrapbook
(In aid of the Royal Photographic Museum)
Romantic Royal Marriages
Barbara Cartland's Book of Celebrities
Getting Older, Growing Younger

Verse:

Lines on Life and Love

Music:

An Album of Love Songs
sung with the Royal Philharmonic Orchestra.

Films:

A Hazard of Hearts
The Lady and the Highwayman
A Ghost in Monte Carlo
Duel of Love

Cartoons:

Barbara Cartland Romances (Book of Cartoons)
has recently been published in the U.S.A., Great Britain,
and other parts of the world.

Children:

A Children's Pop-Up Book: "Princess to the Rescue"

Cookery:

Barbara Cartland's Health Food Cookery Book
Food for Love
Magic of Honey Cookbook
Recipes for Lovers
The Romance of Food

Editor of:

"The Common Problem" by Ronald Cartland (with a preface by the Rt.
Hon. the Earl of Selborne, P.C.)
Barbara Cartland's Library of Love
Library of Ancient Wisdom
"Written with Love" Passionate love letters selected by Barbara Cartland

Drama:

Blood Money
French Dressing

Philosophy:

Touch the Stars

Radio Operetta:

The Rose and the Violet
(Music by Mark Lubbock) Performed in 1942.

Radio Plays:

The Caged Bird: An episode in the life of Elizabeth Empress of Austria.
Performed in 1957.

Videos:

A Hazard of Hearts
The Lady and the Highwayman
A Ghost in Monte Carlo
Duel of Love